LONDON'S BURNING

Also available in Pocket

London's Burning
Blue Watch Blues

London's Burning

FLASHPOINT

A **LONDON'S BURNING** book in association with **LWT**

JOHN BURKE

POCKET BOOKS

LONDON · SYDNEY · NEW YORK · TOKYO · SINGAPORE · TORONTO

A London's Burning Book in association with LWT
Based on the original screenplays by
Brian Elsley, David Humphries, Jane Hollowood,
Roger Marshall and Simon Sharkey
Series producer Paul Knight
The London's Burning series is based on an original film by
Jack Rosenthal
Jacket photograph reproduced by kind permission of LWT

First published in Great Britain by Pocket Books in 1995
An imprint of Simon & Schuster Ltd
A Paramount Communications Company

Simon & Schuster Ltd
West Garden Place
Kendal Street
London W2 2AQ

Simon & Schuster of Australia Pty Ltd
Sydney

A CIP catalogue record for this book is available from the
British Library

ISBN 0-671-85448-8

Typeset in 12/14pt Cochin by
Palimpsest Book Production Limited, Polmont, Stirlingshire
Printed and bound in Great Britain by
HarperCollins *Manufacturing* Ltd, Glasgow

1

George Green had never been very good at making ends meet. Each time he thought he had managed to get things straight, some fresh demand would be made and he would find himself back at the bottom of the ladder. Which was where he was right now. And not a fireman's ladder, which held far fewer terrors for him.

'We've got to get out of here,' Kelly was wailing. 'It's bad enough with just Sean. We can't squeeze another kid in here. And I'm not going to have them poisoned by rats. Or maybe eaten alive.'

'It wasn't a rat,' he said wearily, for what must have been the tenth time. 'It was only a little mouse. Just one. And definitely not a man-eater.'

'Mice, rats – what's the difference? This just isn't fit for any decent person to live in. The wall's damp, and that window leaks.'

The whine in her voice made Sean start crying.

George picked him up, and felt a damp wodge of corn flakes being transferred to his cheek. Looking past the boy's warm head he saw the girl he had taken responsibility for in such a rush. His wife. Every now and then he found that hard to believe. As she leaned against the sink, from one angle she still had that shape he had been so eager to get his hands on, and when she laughed it was just like the sound that had first attracted him that night three years ago. Only nowadays she didn't laugh all that often; and from another angle he could see how that shape was swelling. More responsibilities, more expense, and more complaints. That peevish voice, and the number of things she found to whine about, were beginning to get him down.

Lying awake at night, worrying about money and the sheer business of getting up and breathing and slogging his guts out doing a job, George sometimes wondered how the hell he had got here in the first place.

His father had spent all his working life on the buses, and since marrying had always lived in the same Hackney terrace. Never highly paid and never looking for a better job, Mr Green watched over his income and expenditure very carefully. There was never enough for luxuries: any overtime, bonuses or unexpected surpluses were paid conscientiously into a small Post Office savings account. At Christmas or during school holidays, any few shillings spent on pleasure were doled out so painfully that all the pleasure was stifled from the start. It was not that he was mean: just that some instinctive fear had been burnt into him that next week there might somehow not be another pay packet, so there always had to be a tiny bit in reserve for a rainy day.

As to George's mother, she was loyal to her husband's every pronouncement, which made her shy of showing too much affection to George, in case it made him unreliable. 'Unreliable' – it was the most severe condemnation heard in the Green household. Some of Mr Green's colleagues on the buses were unreliable: late for work, messing whole schedules up because they had taken an unauthorized day off, and then threatening to organize strike action if any attempt were made to discipline them. The newsagent on the corner where Mr Green picked up his morning and evening papers at the same times each day was unreliable because sometimes he got up late, and hadn't got the packages sorted out by the time the shop opened; or had sold out by late afternoon and forgotten to reserve Mr Green's copy.

Unlike most of his colleagues, Mr Green did not turn immediately to the sports pages. He did not bet on football pools or on horses. Football matches were unpredictable; and horses were even less reliable than human beings.

George never intended any open revolt against his father. He respected him and couldn't really disagree with any of his opinions, but was never really comfortable with him. When he left school at sixteen and went into a brewery bottling plant, he felt that he owed himself a few treats at the end of a week, or during holidays. He wasn't going to let himself be caged in one dull little house for the rest of his life. He didn't mind working overtime; but not just to make enough money to build up a Post Office account. He bought a motor-bike, pranged it before he had paid off the hire purchase, and felt jubilant yet at the same time guilty when at last he had cleared the debt and could spend money on himself again. He made good resolves, and was continually bewildered that he couldn't manage to keep them.

Just when he was thinking of getting some little pad of his own, swearing that he would set himself a budget and stick to it, his father was made redundant. Mr Green was still only in his early fifties; but privatization of the buses had meant a flurry of 'rationalization', economies, and wholesale dismissal of long-term employees.

'It's just as well.' Mr Green put a brave face on it. 'Wouldn't want to work with them shysters. Mark my words, standards'll go down. Everything'll go down. No tradition any more. Not one of them with any idea of providing a reliable service. Reliable? They don't know the meaning of the word.'

His redundancy money was just about enough to keep them going, and in due course there was the dole. Only they didn't call it that any more and made you feel ashamed for claiming it, and kept finding new names and new ways of reducing it. George postponed leaving home, and went on contributing to the household. It didn't leave much for himself.

Like many an East End contemporary, he got himself on to the amateur boxing circuit to make a few extra quid. He won a bit, and went through it without being able to explain how. He didn't seem to have spent a lot on taking girls out, or in burger bars and pubs. Yet somehow it slipped away. And it ceased being replaced when he took a bad dive and finished up with a broken nose. His mother cried at his appearance, but could still not bring herself to touch him affectionately. His father said that mixing with the fight fraternity would do him no good: whatever their promises, they were all unreliable, each and every one of them. And as to his job in the bottling plant, with all the brewery takeovers and the redundancies, you couldn't say that was a safe place to be. Not something reliable at all.

What had persuaded him in the end to join the Fire Brigade and end up at Blackwall? Some young men joined the Army for security and the swagger that went with a uniform. Some became policemen. The fire services offered regular money, a career, and reasonably predictable time off. And a certain glamour. Of course you never admitted to that. All the talk was of public service, saving human lives, physical fitness, and not putting on any heroics. But there was a certain something about firemen. Especially, he discovered to his personal pleasure, about George Green.

Girls fell for that battered nose and his slow, sideways grin. And when any of them got too intense, you could drop them by spelling out the awkward working hours, sudden unexpected demands by the Watch, a reorganization of shifts – some of it true, a lot of it not, but anyway convincing and bewildering to anyone outside the Brigade.

Until he put Kelly in the club, and had to marry her.

Which had not played any part in his financial calculations. Having to marry her, living briefly with her mother and sister – whose attitude towards Kelly's husband would certainly have been described by Mr Green as 'unreliable' – and then getting their hands on this scruffy little flat had been an expensive business.

Kelly had never ceased complaining about the flat.

'Falling apart round our ears. I don't like to ask anyone in. Least of all our Carol, with that lovely place of hers up the road.'

'Well, they got the money for it when his old man died, didn't they?'

Kelly would never have dreamt of saying out loud that it might not be a bad idea for Mr Green to pack it in and leave them some money; but her face gave her away as she said: 'It's time *something* happened. Sean's growing up. Needs more room. Somewhere to play. And when this next one comes along . . .'

'All right, all right. If there was any way I could grab cash out of thin air – '

'I'm not stopping here with rats. That's it, George. D'you hear me? That is it.'

'How many more times? It wasn't a rat – just a mouse.'

'I don't care. You've got to do something.'

Without much optimism George phoned the landlord. His doubts were well founded. Mr Coggan liked to contact his tenants at one remove, through the monthly rent collector. Listening to complaints was an unprofitable way of spending the time. As George reeled off the catalogue of miseries, Coggan kept drawing in breath and clicking his tongue as a signal that he was going to interrupt; but George's non-stop harangue made this impossible until he concluded: 'Right. That's it. What are you going to do about it?'

'For a start, there were no mice when you rented the flat. What d'you think I am – Rentokil or something? If your domestic arrangements encourage them, well . . .' Coggan shrugged.

'What're you saying – that we're dirty or something?'

'And what about the rain coming in the roof?' Kelly whimpered. 'And those cracks in the walls, like my husband said. I'm trying to bring up a toddler in this place.'

'Lots of people would be grateful for a nice situation like this, with a very fair rent.'

'It's a shit-hole,' said George.

'Oh, please. The property was in perfectly good repair when you took it on. Any damage to the interior is down to you. And comes out of your deposit.'

'You don't give a toss about your properties, do you? As long as you get your rent at the end of the month.'

'Mr Green, I don't have to take this.' Coggan looked at the sour green stain of damp down the wall, and hastily looked away. 'Look, nobody can call me an unreasonable man. I don't go for your tone of voice, but all the same I'll see what I can do about the roof. No promises, mind. As for the mice, I suggest you clean the kitchen and buy a trap. I'll get my representative to check with you at the end of the month. And let's see – he's due tomorrow anyway, isn't he? Perhaps for once you'll have the money ready for him.'

When Coggan had gone, George said: 'That's it. We'll start looking for another place.'

'But we've got to give a month's notice.'

'Sod that. He'll keep the deposit anyway.'

'We can't just clear off, just like that.'

'I thought you were the one who wanted out of here?'

'Yes, but George, where can we go – and what we goin' to use for money?'

In the mess for the next few days George gave up studying the sports pages, which had been about as useless to him as his father could have predicted, and went through small ads for flats and small terraced houses, and job ads. Neither the Accommodation nor Jobs Vacant columns carried much that was of any use.

On the Sunday, after bathing Sean, he settled down with the local free sheet and the previous evening's paper.

Kelly fidgeted for a while in the nearest thing she could ever get to silence, and then burst out: 'If you're trying to find a winner at Wetherby and losing even more money on a horse that sprains its ankle after a hundred yards – '

'I'm looking for work in the ads, aren't I?'

'George, maybe if you were to be a little more polite to my dad – '

'I'm not going to do any more cut-rate jobs for any skinflint removal man.'

'My dad's not a removal man. He's a light haulage contractor.'

'Light haulage? Him and your brother, they're what I call real heavy going.'

Kelly sulked until early evening, when he took her out for a drink, waiting every minute for her to say that it would be better if they saved their money instead of spending it in pubs. But she met two old friends who were living in a new, smart house on the edge of the park, and insisted that George bought them both a drink just to show that things were going fine for them, too. Only when they got home and he wanted to make love to her did she start sulking again.

Leaving in the morning, he said: 'If that rent collector comes round, don't open the door. Make out you're out.'

'Don't worry. I'm getting well used to that.'

Blue Watch had a busy day: no major outbreaks or dangerous challenges, but a sequence of minor incidents that involved a lot of routine work and one bout of equipment cleaning and reloading after another.

Late in the afternoon they were called to a fire in a pillar-box. It was easy enough to extinguish, but by the time they had finished, all the letters were ruined. A gang of kids made no pretence of being innocent bystanders. They leapt up and down, jeered at the firefighters, and hooted with derision when Sub Officer Hallam swooped and asked if they thought it was funny, destroying other people's mail. Yes, they did regard it as funny.

'Kids!' said Station Officer Georgiadis, sitting in the cab of the pump ladder and scowling down on the scene. 'Makes you wonder why people have them, doesn't it?'

On the driver's side, Sally Reid's dark features

split into a wide, tolerant smile. 'You'll feel differently when you have some of your own, guv.' She leaned out of the window. 'Isn't that right, George?'

'Makes all the difference in the world,' he said glumly.

At the end of the shift, two burly shadows came towards him out of the dusk. 'Got a little job for you, George.'

'Look, I'm not in the market right now.'

His brother-in-law sniggered. 'Hear that, Denzil? Not in the market. Now, that's a good one, eh? Considering. Wait till we tell him what he'll be taking to market.'

'Les, after that last stupid bloody job I told you to find your dogsbody somewhere else.'

'Plenty of time to do it. I know you're off duty tomorrow. Green Watch doing the day shift, eh? We're well genned up on your routine now.'

'I've told you – '

'And we've told Kelly you won't be home till tomorrow morning. But she's not to worry. You're taking two hundred turkeys to Birmingham.'

'But it's nowhere near Christmas. Unless they do things differently in Birmingham.' Then it dawned on him what Les had said. 'Just a sec – what right have you got to go telling Kelly when I'll be home and when I won't?'

'Shouldn't keep putting her in the club if you can't afford to keep her.'

'Who says I can't afford to keep her?'

'I do. Told her there wasn't any money in the Fire Brigade when she married you, George. And d'you know, I just happened to be round seeing her this afternoon when the rent man called. Very upsetting for her. Not the sort of thing I fancied happening to my sister. So I paid him.'

'You did what?'

'Paid him. So let's talk turkey, right?' Les held out a key ring. 'The van's behind the sheds, usual place. And the address and a map are on the seat. You can't go wrong. Or let's hope you can't, just for once.'

The drive was long, steady and boring. George yawned and at intervals rubbed his eyes. Once he was clear of London the evening traffic was not too heavy, but it was slow going around a pile-up outside Birmingham, where a large lorry had shed half its load of potatoes. Turkey and roast potatoes: the thought blended muzzily in George's head with a longing to tell his brother-in-law to get stuffed.

He was half an hour late finding the Handsworth address. The man at the warehouse had been about to give up, and grumbled away to himself the whole time it took them to unload. When they were finished he made it clear that he wanted the van out of the yard without delay.

'All fixed at your end, eh?'

In other words, there was no payment at this end,

not even a tip, not even the offer of a cup of tea and a sandwich.

George was drawn towards the lights of a pub at the junction of a long, slowly curving street and the entrance to a lorry park. He tucked the van close in to the gates, under the sour glow of a sodium street lamp, and slouched in through the side door of the pub.

His luck being the way it was, the welcome was what he might have expected. 'Sorry, mate, last orders over already.' A man in shirt sleeves, with braces tightening across a large belly, gave him one dismissive wave and disappeared through the door behind the bar. A woman collecting glasses and loading them into a washer glanced at George; then looked harder, and appeared to be sorry for what she saw. 'Been hard at it, eh? All right, make it quick. What's it to be?'

Coming straight from the station, and offered nothing in advance by Les, he had only two quid and a few coppers in his pocket. 'A half of bitter and a packet of crisps.'

'A half – or a pint?'

'A half. I'm driving.'

She pulled the half, and kept eyeing him as she wiped the bar. 'Skint?'

'Had to do a rush job. Urgent delivery from London. Left in a hurry without my wallet.'

'You're not going to drive back tonight, are you?'

'Can't afford anything else.'

Three obvious regulars called a slurred 'G'night, Margie' as they dragged their way out of the door. A shabby woman who had been sitting over an empty glass in the far corner blinked, looked round, and then gathered up her bag and a crumpled newspaper, and left.

Margie said: 'Look, there's a bit of today's lasagne left. Won't take a minute to heat up.'

'No, it's all right, I'd best be thinking of – '

'It'll do you good.'

George had been making conversation automatically in a trance of weariness. Now he took a good, straight look at Margie. In daylight those wrinkles round her eyes and mouth might show her real age, but here in the subdued lighting she had the sort of brassy seductiveness that would ensure a regular clientele in the pub – an automatic come-hither smile she could not turn off even at the end of a tiring evening.

When she went out through the door behind the bar, her hips were swaying. When she came back with the lasagne, she looked as warm as the dish itself.

She finished the glasses and set them back on the shelf, glancing at him every few minutes. By the time he had scraped round the edges of the dish, George was feeling relaxed, well clear of the last few dismal hours.

Margie said: 'If you don't fancy driving all the

way back tonight, you could have a kip in our spare room if you like. Bed hasn't been made up, but it's clean enough.'

'That's nice of you, but – '

'Go on. I won't charge.'

She showed him up a narrow twist of staircase, smelling of musty carpet, to a cramped room opening off the half-landing. There was about three feet to spare between a single bed and a window with a flimsy lace curtain.

'You'll be all right?' said Margie.

'I'll be fine, thanks.'

'If you want the window open' – she did not so much brush past him as press languorously against him – 'shove this bit of wood underneath, will you? Otherwise it's liable to come down with a bang.' She made her return journey slowly and even closer. 'I'd better go and finish off.'

When she had gone, George peered out of the window. The street lamp made the curtain look even yellower than it probably was in daylight. Its light caught the roof of the van, parked in the entry, and was echoed by a crescent of lights along what, from here, seemed a tighter curve in the road than was obvious from below.

George collapsed gratefully on the bed. Lights of a car came along the road and sketched a bright path across the ceiling. He closed his eyes. He would have to get up not later than five o'clock. Les would just love to make a fuss if he could claim loss of business because the van had come back late.

The window creaked. The door creaked. He had been half expecting it.

'Care for some company?'

'Look, wasn't that your old man downstairs?'

'He's snoring already. Had a darts match this evening. He always gets legless by the end of the match.'

George was tempted. Kelly hadn't been much in the mood since she'd found herself with another bun in the oven. And in the dim light from the street lamp the woman looked shapely enough. There'd be no problems. She wasn't the kind to present problems. Maybe he wasn't as tired as he had thought.

She was bending over him. Her hair reeked of beer and stale cigarette smoke. He put one arm round her, and willingly she loaded her full weight on to him. She had already undone her blouse buttons.

From some distance away a light began to reach up through the window. It grew brighter, swinging in a long arc towards the corner. The sound of a lorry, going too fast, grew louder, and the lights went on growing brighter and brighter. Margie's greedy face was floodlit as she grinned down at George. At any moment the lorry would racket past and the brilliance would be doused.

It did not take the curve. The lights blazed on

in a direct, unswerving path, and suddenly there was an almighty crash. With Margie beginning to pant on top of him, and then screaming in panic, George could not swear that he felt the earth move; but the floor certainly moved. It came up in several splintering sections, and segments of the wall crunched away to either side. Bits of ceiling showered down. The window shattered and the outer wall opened up to the night air. Framed in the gap was the top of the cab of an artic.

Margie went on screaming, stumbling towards the door. George swung groggily off the edge of the bed, wiping ceiling plaster out of his hair.

Groping down the blacked-out stairs, a panic of his own grabbed him. What about Les's van – could it have been crushed by the oncoming artic?

Somewhere in the back of the pub he could hear Margie still yelling her head off, then the mumble of her husband's voice. George was lost. He groped his way across the bar to find himself facing the offside front wheel of the artic. The driver was unharmed, to judge from the volley of language shooting out from the middle of the tangle. One of the pub doors had been crushed in the impact, and there was no way out in that direction. When he turned away, trying to adjust his eyes to the uncertain light and unfamiliar shapes, George blundered into a narrow passage which proved to be the entrance to the toilets.

Somewhere close at hand a door opened, and the

landlord's voice ranted out. George stayed very still. Arguments about his presence would prove very tricky. Footsteps went past. There was the squeak of bolts being slid back, and a sudden draught. The man had opened the main door on to the street and was lurching round to inspect the damage.

George followed, but ran to the far side of the road and then along under the shadow of a wall until he could get a view of Les's van.

The artic had missed it. There was just enough space to back out, if he could get across without having to answer any awkward questions from Margie's husband. It ought not to be too difficult. A handful of men and women from houses a few hundred yards away were hurrying towards the accident, gaping and clustering round the back end of the artic, sticking out of the perilously leaning end of the pub. It was all too familiar: at any hour of the day or night, in any neighbourhood, rubberneckers were sure to come out like grubs from under a stone.

Something else familiar added itself to the night air. The two tones of a fire appliance were howling closer to the scene, and as George reached the far side of the road the blues flashed into sight.

It was unlikely that anyone from a provincial fire station would recognize him, but you never knew. Firefighters who had transferred from one region to another might by some horrible coincidence remember him. And if some newsreel cameraman showed up on the scene, there was no telling where the results might be shown. Blackwall's White Watch had had to rescue him from a humiliating episode involving a grand piano; and one of the Shadbrook teams had laughed their heads off while putting out a blaze in the mobile burger bar where he had been moonlighting. No, he couldn't risk hanging around here any longer.

Before he could back the van carefully round the end of the artic, a pump had slewed in behind him. Someone was yelling: 'Get that thing out of the way – we need to come in there.' Before anyone could leap down from the cab to tackle him personally, George waved an obedient hand and began edging out. The pump made way for him, and without waiting to thank Margie for her hospitality or apologize for not completing their brief relationship, he was heading towards the M1, wide awake in spite of the traumas of the evening.

It was only when he got back to his father-in-law's yard in the early dawn that he noticed the large dent in the side of the van. A chunk of the pub must have fallen against it. That would take some explaining.

George groaned. Even when it came to a simple unskilled matter of handling crates, or turkeys, or a burger frier, he had a feeling he would never be among the lucky ones. If only he could shrug everything off, ignore money worries, not give a damn. Great to be young and jaunty like Billy Ray, who made the most outrageous advances to one girl after another and yet came out unscathed and free from liabilities. Or like Kevin, a risky gambler who seemed to come up trumps more often than not. Look at that greyhound of his, for a start.

But gambling . . . even if he had fancied his chances, the thought of what Kelly would say when he lost, which he inevitably would . . .

No good. It was too late to be young and feckless like Billy. And he would never have the luck that Kevin had with the cards.

The brighter the light over the rooftops, the worse the dent in the van looked. George turned his gaze wretchedly away, and set out for home.

2

The greyhound had been the spoils of one of Kevin Medhurst's more successful gambles. Growing desperate in the small hours, rubbing his smarting eyes and trying to interpret Kevin's expression through the haze, his opponent had risked everything on one last throw.

The smoke would have been enough to set off any smoke alarm the room might have had, if it had been the sort of room where fire precautions were ever likely to be installed. Interweaving blue tendrils curled up from the card table and snaked around the ceiling.

There had been a long silence. Kevin broke it at last. 'Up to you, Gary? What's it going to be?'

'I've got to stay with it.'

'Fair enough. But you'll have to cover it first.'

Gary's eyes were almost shut. It was too obvious that he hadn't got as much as a fifty-pence piece left. But through the slits of his eyelids he was hypnotically studying the cards in his hand. 'Yeh. Look. I'll . . . I'll put me dog in to cover it.'

Kevin stared, incredulous. 'You *what*?'

'Good pedigree. I've got him in training. He'll cover it.'

'Don't be crazy,' protested Steve, the friend who had set up this session. 'That dog's worth a grand.'

Gary ignored him. 'Kev?'

'We're playing for money, not pets. What would I do with a dog?'

'If you've got any sense,' growled Steve, 'you'll race it, mate.'

'You ready, Kev? A grand?'

'Okay.'

'The dog's on the table. What you got?'

Kevin prolonged the torture, spreading his cards one by one: King of clubs, King of hearts, the four and three of hearts . . . and the King of diamonds. 'Anyone round here got a dog lead?'

Then it became a matter of finding kennels near Blackwall. Billy Ray, of course, knew exactly where to go. A friend whose aunt was married to the director of the local stadium could get him a cut-price deal, only Billy would have to sweet-talk her first – so maybe he could have a few bob to take her out one evening? It would be an investment: accommodation and the services of a kennel boy didn't come cheap, but Kevin would save on this personal introduction, and of course once the winnings started to roll in . . .

'In the meantime' – Kevin was beginning to wonder if he had been wise to accept the dog rather than hold out for cash instalments over a long period – 'I've got to pay for its keep, and entry fees, or whatever.'

'And keep some cash in reserve for when Billy quarrels with this bird of his,' said Sicknote, 'and everything turns sour.'

Billy scowled, but it took more than one remark like that to damp his jauntiness. 'Why not form a company, here in the Watch? Put money in, share out the winnings.'

'If any,' said Sicknote.

He was the only one not to put a few quid in, on the grounds that his wife wanted them to save up for a holiday and didn't like dogs anyway – not since Sicknote had rescued a scruffy mongrel from a City Farm fire and tried to adopt it, assuring her she would grow to love it. Jean had not grown to love it. He wouldn't even risk the mention of another dog.

Kevin basked in the approval of the entire Watch after the greyhound, named Blue Watch after hours of brain-racking discussion, won its first race. And then its second. The entire Watch rejoiced, with the exception of Bert Quigley: Sicknote was, as Bayleaf quietly commented, 'as sick as a dog'.

Life looked very promising; until one evening

when Kevin was getting into his car and there was a timid rap on the window.

It was a face he had hoped not to see for a long time yet; and preferably never. For a moment he was tempted not to wind the window down but to drive off and leave the old no-hoper standing there. Only, he knew what would happen then. An hour or so later that familiar, seedily ingratiating smile would be turned on outside their own front door.

He wound the window down. 'Don't tell me you've scarpered again.'

His father said: 'No, son. They let me out. Straight, I've been released.'

'What for? Couldn't be good conduct.'

'I'm sick.'

'You can say that again. If it'd been me, I'd have thrown the key away that last time.'

'Kev, I know I haven't been much of a father. But can't we be friends now? Now that I haven't got long to go.'

Kevin groaned. What sort of story was it going to be this time, squeezed out like sticky toothpaste? 'Where are you thinking of going, anyway?'

'I've got cancer,' said Mr Medhurst. 'That's why they've discharged me. And I'd like . . . well, to spend me last few days with you and your mum.'

There wasn't much of an answer you could wheel out on the spur of the moment. Silently Kevin leaned over to open the passenger door; and stayed silent all the way back to the flat.

His mother looked apprehensive. It was an expression that years of life with Mr Medhurst had made almost permanent, easing off only slightly during the years without him – when he was serving another of his sentences for petty crime.

Kevin watched as his father slunk towards the battered armchair he always regarded as his own, and lowered himself into it with a sickly smile.

Mrs Medhurst glanced at their son and, as if to stop him bursting out in accusation, said: 'You've got to give him a chance, Kev. He *is* your father, after all. You only get one, you know.'

Oh, yes indeed: Kevin knew that all right. The thought of it had festered in his mind right the way through from his childhood. 'If mum wants you around, all right,' he managed to say. 'But don't expect me to kiss and make up. Because it's not going to happen. Never.'

Mr Medhurst did his best to creep round without being noticed; but then began to try a new line of helpfulness. Kevin could not decide whether to be irritated or reluctantly grateful. It did make things easier that his father should show an interest in Blue Watch – the dog, not the Blackwall team. Kevin had to fit visits to the kennels in with working shifts. It was a help to send messages to the kennel boy via his father and get regular reports back. Also, it kept the old man out of the flat. Maybe it was true what they said about pets being good for sick people. A bond of sympathy was forged. It was just possible that in his last days Jim Medhurst would give his son something pleasant to remember him by.

Then Blue Watch lost a race. And another.

'Turned out unreliable after all,' muttered George Green cryptically.

It made no sense. Kevin went to have a closer look at his greyhound, and found that even the day after the race it was still listless and confused. He tore a strip off the kennel boy, then apologized. The lad had always been loyal, and very affectionate towards the dog. How could it have happened?

'I mean, the way it behaved, you'd have thought it was doped.'

'Well,' said the boy awkwardly, 'I couldn't say for sure, but . . . no, it wouldn't mean anything.'

'What wouldn't?'

'All the regular punters are in there half the time, it's nothing you'd think to mention.'

'Mention it.' Kevin was growing angry again.

It came out hesitantly. The boy had seen Mr Medhurst in the pub on the corner a few times recently with that Charlie Edmunds.

Kevin's heart sank. He knew Charlie Edmunds. Everyone around the track knew Charlie, and knew how he operated.

He went to the *Marquis of Granby*.

'Had a nice result then, Charlie?'

Charlie Edmunds, who had just thrown a tenner on the bar and indicated that drinks should be served to a couple of cronies, looked round. His nose and puffy cheeks with their broken blood vessels sagged into an affable grin. 'Nice, yes.'

'Just can't help winning, can you? Horses, dogs: I don't know how you do it.'

Charlie picked up the tone of voice, but was too sure of himself to be even slightly wary. 'What can I do for you, kid? Got something on your mind?'

'As a matter of fact, I have. You and my old man, for starters. What's it all about, Charlie?'

Charlie smirked. 'Perhaps you'd better ask *him* about that. He is your old man, after all. So far as I'm concerned, he's just a friend. Or acquaintance, sort of.'

'Oh, sure. Down the kennels, down the races, talking to you when you wanted to listen. Or wanted him to listen. That's not friendship – not from you.'

'Business, then.' Charlie shrugged, and waved to the barmaid for a refill. 'You have to do what you can, don't you? Hey, I never thought to ask – you got half the Brigade sitting on your shoulder because you let 'em down, right? Couldn't legislate for them, now could I? Not a welfare state, me.'

'You fixed us, didn't you? The pair of you. You got that no-good bastard to fix our own dog for you.'

'Nothing personal, Kev. They're *all* fixed, sonny. That's the way it works, if you're going to do it at all. If you don't want your boys in blue losing out, then put it to your old man. I mean, we both know what he is, don't we? What else did you expect?'

Kevin knew all right what his father was. But he wasn't going to have it sneered at him by this yob. He grabbed Charlie by the collar, pulled him off balance, and slammed him against the wall. Before the barmaid could do more than yell for the landlord to come on the scene, he had managed to get two fistfuls of rage into Charlie's face, and then topple him over and down to the floor. His right shoe might have done a lot more damage if the landlord and one of Charlie's heftier pals had not come to the rescue, hauled Kevin off, and thrown him out bodily into the street.

He had not finished. That evening he confronted his father, who cringed as if he had been expecting this all along – just as Kevin himself ought to have expected some such thing all along. Of course Mr Medhurst denied all responsibility, but the way his left eye began to water, and the way he sat with his fingers playing a feeble cat's-cradle, was all too familiar both to Kevin and his mother. Mrs Medhurst's head drooped and she began crying, just as she always cried when her husband had been caught out yet again, and when she was making up small parcels to take to him in prison.

Kevin said: 'Get out.'

'Son, I know I've been a bit silly, but you can't – '

'Out. We should never have let you in through that door.'

Mr Medhurst turned to his wife. 'Edie, you're not going to let him – '

'He pays the rent,' she said shakily, 'and looks after me. And holds down a good job. Which is more than you ever did.' She was already on her way to pack a small bag for him.

Jimmy Bolley drew a deep breath and marched through the door in the main gate of the Whitelaw Young Offenders' Institution. He tried to look bland and innocent, stopping at the desk to hand over a portable radio. 'For me brother. Steve Bolley.'

The officer on duty inspected it, removed the battery cover, and prodded the leads. 'Mm. Nice. I'll check it over. He can have it after your visit.'

There was also a plastic bag of chocolates and a few cigarettes.

'Nothing big enough to hide a file in,' said Jimmy chirpily.

The officer managed a condescending grin. It was the sort of remark you got used to after some years of this routine.

The brothers leaned towards one another across the table, but not so closely that any warder plodding around the inmates and their visitors would have reason to suppose anything was being passed between them. The only reason they might have for any suspicion was that Jimmy and Steve were behaving with such blatant innocence. All that passed between them was muttered conversation, most of it when the duty officers had reached the far ends of the room.

'The workshop closes at six,' mumbled Steve. 'It'll take a good hour before the stuff works. But when it goes, I need to know you'll be there.'

A warder came on a route across the room from side to side.

'Mum's worried about that bike of yours,' said Jimmy. 'It'll only rust while you're in here. Should she advertise it in the paper shop window?'

'Maybe that'd be best.' Steve waited for the footsteps to plod away and said: 'You'll be parked in Cuthbert Road, seven sharp?'

'You've checked out you can get to that wall and over?'

'Just get your end right. I'll sort it out inside here.'

When time was up they nodded a resigned, brotherly farewell, and Steve waited for his radio to be handed over. Not that he would get much use out of it. It would be left behind – maybe to get burned up in the flames.

The plan was simple enough – so simple that

either it would work like a dream, or never get off the ground. Either way, there would be no traces of how the thing had started.

When the workshop was due to close, Steve conscientiously swept up the shavings and steered them towards the bin. Instead of scooping them up, he brushed them under a radiator before which he had casually pulled a half-finished firescreen someone had been working on. From his pocket he took the half-pound of lard he had nicked from the canteen and fitted with a length of string. Hanging from the radiator, it would gradually melt, drip on to the shavings, and catch fire. Or if it didn't, the theory would prove a washout, and that would be that – and he would have to get to the evidence as soon as possible in the morning and get rid of it.

He went back to his cell and stretched out, fully clothed and alert.

The waiting was the worst of it. At the end of what he thought must have been a half-hour, he found that five minutes had passed. He began gnawing his left thumbnail until he had torn a long slice of it away. All the sounds were the same as ever: feet clanking along the landing, somebody clattering up the metal stairs, and somebody playing a radio in the next cell. He had not dared switch his own new set on, in case he missed some significant noise that would trigger the plan into action.

At last there was the jangle of a fire alarm. It went on for quite some time before steps went past his door and somebody was shouting: 'That bloody thing playing up again. Check it, and fix it.' Another interminable minute, and at last it came: 'It's real! Fire! Get 'em out.'

The bells went down. The two appliances swung out of the Blackwall bay and raced towards the ugly block of the detention centre. Smoke was curling round the inner buildings and beginning to drift over the outer wall. The leading pump jarred to a halt before the imposing double doors, with only one small opening at the side. A warder stood waiting for them.

Station Officer Georgiadis leaned out of the cab, ready to ask how the hell they were supposed to cope if the gates remained bolted against them, when the two wings shuddered back, and a warder jumped on to the step of the pump. 'I'll show the way. Turn under that arch in the yard – pull round the moment you're inside.' As they slowed under the arch, he added: 'One man injured inside. Got kicked halfway down the main staircase. And there's a lot of smoke in there.'

The inner yard was filled with wildly dancing prisoners, jeering and howling with delight. They roared at the flames, urging them on. Not that the fire needed any encouragement. It must have funnelled up the centre hall, and was already dancing out of upper windows, which only encouraged the young men to dance even more deliriously.

Georgiadis made a quick appraisal. 'Bayleaf, drive us close against that side wall. Pearce, Recall – get your B.A.s on and see about that officer inside, on one of the stairways. Sub, the main hydrant's by that window. And get the hoses started at that end.' He sprang down, made another brief assessment, and shouted to the driver of the second appliance: 'George, on the blower. Make pumps four.'

Getting through the jubilant crowd was almost as tricky as coping with the fire. The handful of warders tried to control the riotous inmates, but they surged to and fro, tripped over hoses, and were certainly in no mood to get out of the way while the firefighters tried to save the prison.

Georgiadis thought he glimpsed one young man racing towards the pump against the inner wall, but he disappeared in the thickening haze. One or two of the demonstrators were beginning to cough violently, losing some of their early elation.

Bayleaf ran round from the driver's seat of the pump to roll up the shutter and reach for his helmet and protective gear. A hand fell on his shoulder, he dropped the helmet; and a fist smacked hard down on his head, sending him reeling along the side of the appliance with pain scouring his cheek until he fell and hit the ground.

Steve Bolley dragged the helmet and uniform on as he sprinted through the arch. As he neared the outer gate, wide open now, he slowed to a businesslike walk. A distant two-tone announced the approach of back-up engines. If he kept it steady, he would look like one of the crew preparing to report conditions to the new arrivals.

Behind him there was a shout. 'A runner! We've got a runner!'

Steve tried not to panic. He kept to his measured pace, looking straight ahead as he passed the guardroom. But the radio in there was blasting out its message full power. 'A runner – in firefighting gear. Police!'

It was a voice to carry hundreds of yards. His brother must have heard it. A car started up beyond the wall and accelerated wildly; and as Jimmy Bolley drove off into the night, two warders and a policeman were pouncing on Steve, forcing him brutally against the edge of the gate and then back inside.

It was not until two days later, when they had all been shifted to other locations around London, that he heard Jimmy was dead – killed in a crash as he drove recklessly round a corner to escape a pursuit that everybody had in fact been too busy to start.

There was another death, less spectacular. Kevin learned that his father had died, in the dismal little room he had found for himself in a Hoxton boarding-house. The caretaker wanted his effects out of the way in a hurry: that battered little bag, and a manilla envelope addressed to Kevin which Mr Medhurst had never got round to posting.

The envelope contained several hundred pounds – his winnings on Charlie Edmunds' dog which he had helped to win those last two races.

Kevin wanted to feel remorse, or affection. Too late: it wouldn't come. It made better sense to keep himself protected, armoured against emotion regarding anyone who had been such a dead loss. No emotion other than dull disgust would fit the bill.

Stony and dry-eyed, he gave his mother half the cash, shared out the rest between the Blue Watch backers – 'Your investment back, with interest,' he said flatly – and announced that the dog was going back to its original owner. Nobody argued. They knew little of what had happened, other than his father's death, but raised no questions. There were times to let fly with mutual mockery in the station, and times to stay quiet and steer clear. This was one of the times for quietness, giving him room to breathe and get back to normal.

It was only after a tactful lull that Recall asked casually: 'How's your mum taking it, Kev?'

'She'll be a country girl at the end of the month. Wants to move in with her sister now the old man's gone.'

'Whereabouts is that?'

'Southend.'

'That's not the country.'

'All right, the seaside, then.'

'It's a council flat, isn't it?' said Sub Officer Hallam. 'So where does that leave you – homeless?'

'I'll have to start looking.'

Sicknote, green with envy over the handout and anxious to stir up whatever could be stirred, perked up. 'Sally, you've been looking young Kevin over recently. Fancy putting him up?'

'If it's a choice between you and him . . .' Sally Reid shrugged contemptuously.

Things were back to normal.

3

Most of the tables in the restaurant were occupied by couples, with a few groups of four or six gathered around bottles of retsina, showing signs of growing noisier as the evening wore on. Nick Georgiadis had chosen a small table in one of the alcoves. It was an ideal intimate setting for a loving couple; but Nick ate alone, as he had done for several weeks now.

His Uncle Dimitri propped himself against one of the alcove panels and said: 'So. You feel sorry for yourself.'

'Not specially.' Nick did not look up.

'But you do feel sorry. What did I tell you?'

'Go on,' said Nick wearily. 'Sing it again. I was a fool to let her go, right?'

'Right. Ariadne, she is to marry. She will have babies. She is happy.'

'Great. I don't want babies in my life right away.

If she's happy, I'm happy for her.'

'So you go for the boss's daughter instead. And where is she now?'

Nick was tempted to say that he didn't give a damn where either of them was now. It would not have been strictly true. Somewhere something had gone wrong, but he wasn't going to give Uncle Dimitri the chance to gloat. He had let Ariadne slip through his fingers rather than be tied down; yet now remembered the touch of her hand and the way she had of murmuring, almost singing, his name when she was in his arms. But she was engaged, and that was that. With Diana it had looked like it would work out in spite of the embarrassment of finding she was Commander Bulstrode's daughter, and he had felt that this time he was ready for a commitment – only to find that she was the one who didn't want it. But sorry for himself? Absolutely not. A bit perplexed, but not giving in to maudlin regrets.

He raised his head and said: 'One thing I'd be grateful for.'

'Yes?' Uncle Dimitri hopefully prepared to hear a remorseful confession.

'Have you got any room at the back for my motor-bike? I've just bought myself a car, and there's no parking space in our street for both of them.'

'So you sell the bike.'

'Not yet. I'd rather like to stow it away somewhere

safe for the time being, and use it when I'm in the mood.'

'Such strange moods you have.' Uncle Dimitri sighed and gave up. 'You can try Cousin Yanni. He has that lock-up shed at the bottom of his garden – there is a way in from the path at the back. And he is closer to your flat than this place is.'

'Thanks. I should have thought of that.'

Uncle Dimitri's expression as he walked away suggested that there were many things Nick ought to have thought of before now.

He finished his solitary meal and rode off to Yanni's house. There was an Audi which he did not recognize in the drive. When he rang the doorbell, the door was opened to him by Ariadne, dressed to go out – and to go somewhere smart, by the look of her.

They stared at each other, mute for a moment. Then she whispered: 'Nick, I didn't know you were coming here this evening.'

'I was just hoping to scrounge some garage space for the bike.' He looked past her at Yanni and the man who was moving forward to take her arm possessively.

He could almost hear Uncle Dimitri's sorrowful accusation: This is the man who will soon have what *you* could have had.

'Hello, Petros.'

Petros's response was too loud and too cordial. 'Hello, Nick. We would have a drink together, but we are dining out, you see.' He made a point of drawing Ariadne closer.

'Yes, I see.'

Yanni said: 'I hear something about your bike, Nick?'

'Yes, Uncle Dimitri suggested you might – '

'A moment. Petros, you have forgotten our little parcel.'

The two men turned back for a moment into the hall.

Ariadne breathed: 'I'll call you.'

'Easier if you didn't.'

'I'll call you,' she insisted, just before Petros came back and again took her arm and led her towards the Audi. Yanni stood watching them go. Nick made a point of looking away, patiently waiting until they could talk about his bike.

Blue Watch's first call the next evening was a simple one, and they were back in the station before eight o'clock. Sally Reid was waiting in the watchroom to intercept the station officer on his way through.

'A.C.O. Bulstrode is in your office, guv.'

'Wonder what he wants this time of day?' said Billy Ray. 'Thought his sort was always out at masonic meetings or golf club dinners in the evenings.'

Leading Firefighter Geoff Pearce could not resist the opportunity to pontificate. 'Commander Bulstrode's your superior officer, Billy. What he wants is no concern of yours. Just get your gear off and see about rustling up some dinner.'

Nick went briskly up the stairs. 'Sorry to keep you waiting, sir, but we've been on a shout.'

'So I heard. What was it?'

'House – couple locked themselves out.'

'Are they going to pay?'

'The husband signed the form.'

'Hmph. That makes a change. Most people baulk at the thought of paying for our services. That'll be the next thing, you know. Management consultancy will suggest we're privatized, and the public will be charged for everything we do. Sort of pay as you burn.'

'I take it you've just come from H.Q., sir. Shall I have some tea sent up?'

'Tea?' Bulstrode glanced at the wall clock and then at the desk. 'Gone are the days when the station officer kept a secret supply of Scotch.'

'Long gone, sir.'

It was the first time that Nick had been conscious of the A.C.O.'s advancing age. There were echoes in Bulstrode's name which had always resonated perfectly: a large bull of a man, he exuded confidence and an aura of physical strength which no one in the lower ranks could hope to match. Yet now his body was puffy rather than strong and his face seemed to have drooped, not just with the strain of a troublesome day but with something deeper and more lasting.

'Well, as you'll have guessed,' he said, as if it were almost too much of an effort to speak, 'I had a meeting with the top brass this afternoon. A long meeting. Main topic being Tuesday's incident at the prison. They want to know what the hell happened, and why.'

'My report's on its way to you, sir. You ought to have had it by now.'

'Probably sitting in my office while I'm fending off the pinpricks elsewhere. I look forward to reading it. Lines have been buzzing with Blackwall's name. Brigade uniform taken in an escape. Two men injured in a car crash, and one relative of the escaper killed.'

'Only the man didn't escape, sir.'

'No, didn't quite make it. But he managed to attack a firefighter and grab that uniform. The press have had a field day. Anyway, the message from H.Q. is this: if there's any egg left flying about after this incident, it had better not land on our faces.'

'I'm satisfied that all orders were followed correctly, sir.'

'Hmph. How is Wilson?

'He's at home, getting some rest.'

'We'll have our own debrief, of course. Apparently that's not good enough. Top brass want to appoint a D.O. to take part in a . . . a review of procedure regarding secure units.'

'Anyone we know, sir?'

'Hotfoot from north-east area. They haven't confirmed it yet. Knows a bit about prisons, apparently. You know, the only fireman I've ever come across who knew anything about prisons had done time for bigamy.' Bulstrode laughed at his own joke, but without real enjoyment. Abruptly he barked, more in his old style: 'Our friends at H.Q. are interested to note that Firefighter Wilson is the same chap who crashed an appliance some little while ago. Has he got a death wish or something? Or does he want to get out of the Brigade early on medical grounds?'

'Wilson is one of our most capable and long-serving firefighters, sir.'

'Sadly, length of service doesn't seem to count for very much in the Brigade these days, Georgiadis.'

If there were more to be said, he evidently decided it was advisable not to say it, and with his characteristic 'Hmph' headed for the stairs. On the way down he turned aside through the mess. The Watch began scrambling to their feet.

'Don't let me disturb you, gentlemen. That was a nasty shout around that prison. But it might have been much worse. Well done, all of you.'

'Thank you, sir.' Geoff Pearce was quick to appoint himself as spokesman. Nick felt the hackles rise on his neck at the mere sound of that unctuous voice. 'Would you like something to eat while you're here, sir?

'No, thank you. I have to be on my way. Goodnight.' About to get into his car, he said to Nick: 'Must phone Jenny. Another ruined dinner.'

'How is Mrs Bulstrode, sir?'

'Fine. A bit worried about Diana now that she's got that flat of hers. Though Diana seems fine, too. If you're interested.'

Nick wondered how interested he might be again, given the opportunity.

It was a subject which cropped up again within a few days. In spite of his warning, Ariadne phoned, breathless and insistent that she must see him, and not giving him time to disagree. They met for lunch in a riverside restaurant as remote from the tightly knit Greek community's regular haunts as it was possible to get without driving to the Welsh border.

She was very simply dressed in a crisp white blouse and terra-cotta skirt. Her raven-dark hair was woven into a tight, gleaming bonnet around her head, pulled well back from her high forehead.

She stared at him long and hard across the table and said: 'Are you sorry to see me?'

'Don't talk nonsense.'

'You do not look happy.'

'I don't have to. You're the one who's supposed to be looking happy. Ecstatic young bride-to-be. Whirlwind courtship, plush wedding, happy ever after.'

'I am not ecstatic. And I am not young.' She sat silent while he ordered, and after a sip of wine she stared at him even more intently. 'You haven't seen Diana recently?'

'Didn't seem to be much point, after what we said to each other. It could only get worse.'

'She's like you. She pleases herself.'

'Is that why you introduced us?'

'I thought she would be good for you.'

'You thought wrong.'

'I'll give up matchmaking in future.'

'I would, if I were you. You're not very good at it.'

Ariadne smiled wistfully into her glass. 'No. Not even for myself.'

'Everybody seems to think it's a wonderful match.'

'Everybody except me.' Again she paused as a small shell of Coquilles St Jacques was set in front of her. When the waiter had gone she picked up a fork but sat there twiddling it, not eating. 'Oh, Nick, I just don't know how I got myself into this. It shouldn't have been anything more than a holiday romance. That's blatantly obvious now that he's here. It was great in Cyprus, on holiday. He was so charming and everything was warm and amusing. It seemed to make things . . . well . . . uncomplicated. Which was a welcome change.'

He felt the sting of the barb, but made a show of eating and looking only politely sympathetic.

'I suppose I should have known better,' she went on. 'But when he asked me . . .'

'Before you knew it, it was wedding dresses and guest lists.'

'Oh, endless guest lists. Part of me wants to go through with it. At least give it a chance. I mean, basically he's a worthy man. I think.'

'Worthy? He looks a bit bossy to me.'

'Perhaps that is what I need?' Ariadne tried the scallops, a slow forkful at a time. 'Very nice,' she said abstractedly. 'But . . . oh, the truth of it is, I don't have much in common with Petros. Not his fault. Just a different world. I'm only just beginning to realize how different.'

'Does anybody else know this?'

'Of course not. They'd go berserk. The wedding's in two weeks. Yet perhaps they are becoming slightly afraid. Already they are . . . closing in around me. Petros has heard I used to see you, and wants to know if I still do. I should not even speak to you if we meet. I am his fiancée, and I must stay . . . stay in purdah. Not meet any old friends, or people will talk. It'll be the same once we're married, I know that already. And Yanni, watching me every moment and telling me as my godfather that I must obey what he tells me and put you out of my mind.'

'So you at once decide to see me, just to put them in their place.'

'It's not like that.'

'What's it like, then?'

She put her fork down despairingly. 'You don't

want to listen, do you? Don't want to hear what I'm really saying. I don't know why I thought I might . . . we might . . .'

'What can I say?'

'I know what you *should* have said. Years ago. None of this would have happened if we . . . if . . .' She was weeping slow, silent tears. He wanted to reach out suddenly and take her hand and let his mask of stoicism crack. But it would have been fatal. 'Don't you ever think about it?'

'Yes. I do. I do think about it.'

He realized at once that this was as dangerous as touching her consolingly would have been. She was imploring him with her moist, shining eyes: 'But if you do think about it, then why . . . Nick, it was you that wouldn't marry me.'

'A bit late for that now.'

It sounded callous, but he had to make a hasty withdrawal before it was too late, and make it sound that way. Things were beginning to hurt behind his mask. Perhaps he had never really had a look in a mirror at his own face and tried to interpret it honestly instead of disguising it.

The two of them looked as though they had been hanging about, waiting for him to show up at the station. When he had parked and was walking back towards the front of the building, Pearce and the woman beside him were still there, just outside the main entrance.

'Evening, sir.'

'Good evening, Geoff.'

'This is my wife, Patti. Patti, this is Station Officer Georgiadis. You've heard me talk about him.'

'Oh, yes. I certainly have.'

Patti Pearce held out her hand. Nick found it soft and limp; and her eyes, though attractively dark and shadowy in the early evening haze, struck him as deceitful. It was an immediate reaction, and probably a silly one.

'Glad to meet you,' he said as warmly as he could.

'The wife's just been shopping, sir.' Pearce put his arm round her shoulder. Nick could have sworn that she flinched; but still she was coyly widening and then half closing her eyes. 'Thought she'd walk along with me and take a quick look at where I and the lads work. Just a look, of course. Mustn't let the general public on Brigade premises, eh?'

'I've heard so much about you.' Mrs Pearce steadied her gaze and looked almost capable of shoving her face right into Nick's. 'Geoffrey does think so highly of you. Needs a strong man to run a strong team, he always says.'

'They're a good bunch.'

'And the deputy has to be up to it, too. That'll be a sad loss, won't it?'

'What will?

'Well . . . John Hallam. When he leaves for his new job. Though I'm sure you'd be the last one to blame him. There comes a time when you know it's right to take a good look at things, doesn't there? Geoffrey was the same at Bristol. He had to make a move to try and get on. Though,' she said meaningly, 'at least he's staying in the Brigade. And perhaps this'll open up the promotion ladder? I'm sure you must have thought about it.'

'I think it's time we went on duty,' said Nick dourly.

'Ooh, have I said something out of order? I mean, it was just chatting to Sandra Hallam in the supermarket, and *she* wouldn't have been telling me things that weren't true, would she? I mean,' Patti Pearce simpered, 'Geoffrey and I wouldn't listen to any old gossip, now would we?'

'I'm sure you wouldn't.'

'But . . . oh, dear, hasn't John got round to telling you yet?'

He stared at her. It really was incredible that Poison Pearce should have a wife just as creepy as himself.

4

Sandra brushed vigorously over his shoulders, down the back, and then started again from the top.

'Look,' John Hallam protested, 'I'm only going to see Peter. He's not going to be any more impressed by me now than he ever was.'

'Don't be silly. There's lots of others you'll be meeting. You do want to look the part. You never know, you might bump into the boss.'

'I think the boss lives in Tokyo. Not much chance of bumping into him in Canary Wharf.'

'Yes, well, whoever. Now's your chance to get somewhere instead of being sub officer for ever. You've got to make the most of it.' Sandra walked round him, eyeing him more favourably than she had done for a long time. 'You've got executive written all over you. Go on, then. And smile a lot. They like that.'

'Who do?'

'The Japanese, of course. It's a Japanese company. 'There're bound to be some about.'

Hallam took a surreptitious glance at his unusually smart self in the hall mirror, and set off. It was a great day for Sandra, and he supposed it ought to have been the same for him. She had so often railed at him about his job – the hours, the strain, the dangers that had once driven him to the verge of a nervous breakdown. She had been so happy when he told her about Peter Whale's invitation; and he wanted her to stay that way. Of course she was right. At last a chance of getting out of the everyday perils of the Brigade, and settling into a comfortable well-paid job: regular hours, civilized surroundings, and the possibility of an even more profitable future. Yet already he felt lukewarm about the whole business. Crazy, but the prospect he dreaded most was having to hand in his notice at Blackwall: the thought of Station Officer Georgiadis's face, and the incredulous faces of the Watch . . .

His doubts were fuelled by the sight of the bleak white tower where he would have to work if this crucial interview finalized the whole thing. Jonah's relaxed, coaxing voice on the phone had given no idea of the scale of the place. Its hundreds of identical windows looked like those in a child's unimaginative stack of building blocks. A muddy-smelling breeze fretted across a stark paved area.

Every day, getting off at the same station or, if he were on that executive level, parking in an officially decreed slot, the routine would be the same. Safe, comfortable; but the same.

Some of his doubts were dispersed when Peter Whale met him in the great glass cage of the foyer and shook his hand with such genuine enthusiasm. They had worked together on a number of Fire Investigation Unit enquiries, and it was flattering that the often cynical Station Officer Whale – known throughout the region as Jonah – should have come to trust him and call for his services from time to time. Now, out of the Brigade himself, he had called on John Hallam again and seemed in no doubt about the outcome.

There were two changes in Jonah's appearance. Firstly, in his civilian clothes he was indistinguishable from other men bustling importantly to and fro between the lifts and the arc of the reception desk, except that he was older than most of them. And secondly, he was balancing himself between two metal crutches.

'Thirty years in the Brigade without a scratch, and then I have to go and do this' – he tapped the left crutch against his shoe – 'getting out of a car. Ah, well, you know what the prophet Isaiah said.'

'No, I don't. But I'm sure you're going to tell me.'

Jonah beamed. '"I have chosen thee in the furnace of affliction." A good choice, too. You'd better be prepared to be my right hand. Or left leg, or whatever. And then there was that remark of Ralph Waldo Emerson's . . .'

Clearly Jonah had brought his quotations dictionary along with him, and would work his way through it as the months went by.

The private security group to which he had chosen to shift occupied two vast floors of the tower. From inside, the windows were more spacious than they had seemed from outside, offering wide, dizzying views over the river, the docklands and beyond. Better than looking down into an inferno from the top of a ladder, Hallam told himself. Yet he felt a more unsettling vertigo here than he had ever felt when the turntable spun and the smoke and flames were raging below.

He turned to look back across the interminable floor. This view was not much better. The mottled sandy carpet actually seemed to slope away into the distance; and clinging to it at very neat, rigidly consistent angles was a sequence of low partitions, within each of which was a desk, a computer, and a young man or woman crouched – at identical angles, too – towards the screen.

'Right,' said Jonah cheerfully. 'In here.'

He led the way round the ends of three partitions and into a space marginally larger than most of the others. It held two desks, with a third just outside in what resembled a sentry-box, in which a trim girl with trim blonde hair was punching data on to her keyboard. Her daffodil yellow blouse and dark green skirt were identical with those of the other girls Hallam had noticed on his way through. She had the same desk space and, he suspected, the precisely measured same knee-room under the desk.

'Anything we deal with comes through Brian's office, over there.' Jonah was pointing to a cubicle distinguished by a glass surround. '*We* are ensconced in here for the present. First recipients of complaints of security lapses at stores we have contacts with. Soothing noises in immediate response, and then you'll be the troubleshooter who sets off and takes the place apart. Analysing defects, looking for the omissions and dodges, and folks cutting corners – the sort of thing you've always been so good at. And then Jenny does the donkey-work, and puts it on record. And holds your hand if things go wrong.' Jenny turned to smile mechanically at Hallam. 'Yes,' Jonah went on, 'she's a gem. A real gem.'

He sounded just as pleased with things as when he had operated from that cramped little F.I.U. office. Maybe he had all along been a man with a liking for compact little burrows. John Hallam doubted his own ability to adjust.

'My desk. Your desk.' He caught Hallam's gloomy appraisal. 'Yes, well, it's not as big as it might be. But there's a move on the cards. Now, let's see if Brian's busy.'

Brian was busy.

'Well, we can always look in after we've had a coffee. Remember what Cobbett had to say about tea and coffee? Never mind, we can't all brew our own beer nowadays.' With which obscure remark Jonah swung on his crutches and headed for the far wall. 'Machine's over this way.'

Back on duty at Blackwall, Hallam felt a lot more comfortable in uniform than he had done in his charcoal grey suit. But it would only be for a while. Jonah had promised to contact him the moment a decision had been reached, but after a brisk five minutes with Brian it had looked unlikely that he would be turned down. He tugged at his collar. Now it was just a matter of waiting a day or two, and then deciding when and how to break it to Georgiadis.

And how would the others take it?

He glanced round the familiar faces in the mess. All part of a family – and just as quarrelsome, supportive, or moody as members of any family.

George was moaning about his wife moaning. Bayleaf was looking uptight, waiting to repel any more remarks about the way his head kept getting in the way of hard objects. Kevin, after a week of lodging with Billy, was loudly asserting his intentions regarding the essential cleanliness and tidiness standards of the place he must soon find for himself. Recall was lamenting the unruliness of his older son Ben, who seemed to be playing truant more and more frequently, and resenting the attention the Mackenzies had to pay to their younger boy, Jamie, because of his fragile condition.

The only moderately cheerful member of the Watch was Sally Reid. Carrying a plate back to the serving hatch, she looked sympathetically down at Recall. 'Has Ben ever tried swimming? The pool's not all that far from your place.'

'He used to enjoy it, when Laura went with him. But she doesn't have much time nowadays.'

'Because of Jamie? Just so. But if he'd like to come along some afternoon, I'm there pretty regularly. I could try getting him interested – set up a few junior competitions later on, or something.'

As Hallam went to check on the watchroom, the phone began to ring. He nodded, said 'On her way', and went back to the mess. Not worth bothering the station officer: it was a decision he could make himself. 'Rotherhithe needs a standby driver. Sally, your turn, by my reckoning.'

'Oh, sub. They've got a very grotty . . . er . . .'

'The lady sub, you mean? Don't be disrespectful.'

'Leave that to the rest of us,' said Sicknote.

'Sicknote, book Sally out. And you man the pump ladder.'

'No rest for the wicked, is there?' said Sally with a melodramatic sigh.

Kevin studied her. 'You're not wicked, are you?'

'Wanna bet?'

His gaze followed her as she hurried off to collect her holdall and jam a long-peaked baseball cap on her head.

She had to step aside at the entrance to the yard as a car swung in. Hallam, looking down from the first landing, gulped. It must be a hallucination. It couldn't be that dreadful character, back from the dead – or back, anyway, from Siberia – after all these years. Couldn't be; and yet it was. Scase. And now with all the trimmings of a D.O.

He put his head round the station officer's door. 'Trouble, guv. Real trouble.'

He set off down the stairs.

Sicknote had emerged to meet the newcomer. 'Firefighter Quigley, on duty in the watchroom, sir. Pump and pump ladder available. Station Officer Georgiadis in charge. Sir.'

'On the ball, are we, Quigley?' Scase's voice was still the same after all this time: a rasp like fingernails dragging across an enamel washing-up bowl. 'Let's see, shall we? Turn your appliances out for drill.'

'Sir.' Sicknote set the bell jangling as Hallam reached the appliance bay, and heard Georgiadis coming down hotfoot behind him.

Bayleaf was at Hallam's shoulder. He too recognized the ogre from the past. 'Gawd. How long has he been a D.O.?'

'Long enough to get a stop-watch, anyway.'

'Looks more like a revenge mission than a drill to me.'

'He'll be looking for clean fingernails, believe me.'

Station Officer Georgiadis had marched forward to introduce himself. Scase nodded without any hint of civility, and glared at the Watch as they lined up for roll-call.

Hallam intoned: 'Leading Firefighter Pearce.'

'Sir.'

'Firefighter Wilson.'

'Sir.'

'Firefighter Mackenzie.'

'Sir.'

'Firefighter Quigley.'

'Sir.'

It droned mechanically on, finishing with Billy Ray.

'Stand at ease.'

'Right. Personal equipment. Let's have a look at that, shall we?' Scase eyed Billy. 'Perhaps we can start with you, Firefighter Ray.' He was good at memorizing names when he planned trouble. After a pleased smile which boded no good, he prowled along the rest of the line like a sniffer dog in search of drugs or explosives. At the end he drew himself up and announced: 'Two items of personal equipment missing on Firefighter Ray. Otherwise all correct. Haven't lost them, I trust, Firefighter Ray?'

'No, sir. They're in my other tunic, sir.'

'Good. That's twenty seconds on your drill time, unfortunately. Now – let's see if the B.A. tallies check with the nominal roll board, shall we? After that you're home and dry.'

Quigley stood to attention by the pump ladder and stared straight ahead, snapping out the words with military precision: 'Firefighter Reid, sir.'

'No you're not, you're Quigley. Or that's what you told me. Who's Reid?'

Georgiadis said: 'She's not here, sir. She's just been sent on standby duty at Rotherhithe.'

'That's right.' Sicknote was still staring stiffly ahead and chopping sentences into slices. 'She left. Just before you came in, sir. I'm manning the pump ladder. I haven't done the B.A. change yet.'

'Oh, dear,' Scase gloated. 'Incorrect B.A. tallies. Another twenty seconds on your time. Just not Blackwall's day, is it?'

He signalled to the station officer that they should go upstairs to the office.

Hallam watched them go, his stomach churning over. With creatures like Scase around, he would be well off out of Blackwall and all it stood for.

'What was it all about?' Billy was awestruck. 'He really had it in for us.'

Hallam explained. Scase had been station commander when Tate was station officer here at Blackwall. Tate had countermanded one of his orders, and Scase never got over it. There was a furious exchange of accusations and counter-accusations; but Commander Bulstrode had stood by Tate and reprimanded Scase. He had been moved soon after – 'to Siberia', as anywhere remote from the London stations was always known.

'Like Captain Bligh and the Bounty,' added Bayleaf, 'bound to show up again.'

'Now he's got Zorba to pick on.' Billy glanced towards the stairs. 'Wonder how *that* will work out?'

Scase stood up from the station officer's desk and handed Georgiadis his Form 9A. 'Copy to the area commander, of course. Publication in the list. Rather a long way down the list, unfortunately.'

'Yes, sir,' said Georgiadis steadily. 'Thank you, sir.'

Scase, well pleased with the day's work so far, made his way out of the office and down the stairs. He was intercepted on the way by Geoff Pearce.

'Can I get the mess manageress to make you a cup of tea, sir?'

'No, thank you, er . . .' This was one name Scase had not yet taken in.

'Pearce, sir. Leading Firefighter Pearce, sir. You wouldn't know me, sir. I transferred up from Bristol, sir.'

'Did you?' said Scase curtly. 'Very enterprising.'

After he had gone, Sicknote sniffed and said, 'Funny smell round here, Geoffrey.'

'Not your nose, is it?' added Bayleaf.

Georgiadis came back from the yard in a rage. 'Billy, in my office. And you, Sicknote.' He could hardly wait for them to get in through the doorway before bursting out: 'Do you know what the average time for a turn-out drill is? Under twenty seconds. We're going on the list at three times that, thanks to you pair. It's going to look more like an advance booking than a turn-out.'

'He could have parked in the yard and given us a chance to spot him,' complained Billy. 'He was gunning for us, wasn't he?'

'He was doing his job. Which is more than you were doing, standing there gawping at him. What d'you do – leave your brain in your other tunic as well?' He swung towards Bert Quigley. 'And what did you do with *yours*? Book it out when Sally went?'

'She was hardly out the gate before he turned up, guv.' Sicknote hesitated, then said, 'My fault, guv. I'm sorry about that.'

'Not half as sorry as I was, watching it happen. Forget procedure enough, you'll kill somebody. Probably one of us. Does that sound good to you?' There was a long pause. Then he grunted; 'Go on. Get back to work.'

Sandra answered the phone, beamed, and said,

'Lovely to hear from you, Peter. Everything working out? Mm. Yes, he's here.' She held the receiver out delightedly to her husband.

John Hallam took it with some trepidation. But the news was what he had wanted to hear. Or at any rate what he had expected. Now he was no longer dangling in mid-air. It was settled.

He saw Sandra's eyes on him, expectant and impatient.

'Great news, Peter,' he said. 'When do I start?'

'How soon can you make it? I need you.'

'Well, I've got to give the Brigade a month's notice, remember.'

'No way of wangling round that?'

'Look, it's not so long since you quit. You know the routine. But I'll try and sort something. I'll get all the bumf filled out and back to you as soon as poss.'

The moment he replaced the phone, Sandra was clinging to his arm. 'Well? When *do* you start the job?'

'You heard me. As soon as I can get out of the Brigade.'

'Better get cracking, then.'

'Yes, well.' He wanted time to sit down and take it all in. 'I'll have to think about it.'

She let go of his arm and stared incredulously. 'What's there to think about? You just hand your notice in. I mean, don't just hang around. Peter'll want to get things moving.'

'All right, all right. I told him I'd sort it.'

'Then start sorting. Anyone'd think you didn't want the job. You still haven't got round to filling in that form he gave you.'

'No, I haven't. And you nagging isn't going to make me do it any sooner. I'll do it when I'm good and ready. In the meantime, please stop hassling me about it.'

Her happiness was fading fast. 'Oh, that's right. As usual. Just waffle about, don't make a decision, and let another opportunity slip away. I know what'll happen. They'll offer the job to somebody else, and you'll be stuck in the same old job for another five years.'

'Just leave it out, will you? I'm beginning to wish I'd never heard about the bloody job.'

Sandra stared at him with mounting disquiet.

5

The afternoons were lengthening. There was a touch of spring in the air when Blue Watch stood down at six o'clock. Nick, who had put his car in for a service and switched back to his bike for a few days, inhaled a heartening scent from Yanni's flowerbeds as he took off his helmet and stowed it into the saddlebag. He opened the shed door and wheeled the bike into the gloom. Shapes of a bench and a cluster of garden tools were faintly visible in the dusky daylight through the window, which added its own duskiness of grime.

There was the faint swish of footsteps across the grass. As he turned, Ariadne came in and dragged the door shut behind her.

Nick stared at her outline and the faint, pale contours of her face in the shadows. 'What are you doing here?'

'Uncle Yanni tells me I don't need to pay the

rest of the rent on my flat. He has invited me to stay with him until the wedding.'

'Invited you? Or ordered you?'

'He is growing suspicious.'

'Only if you make him that way. Good God, dashing down the garden to meet me like this, how's that going to strike him? And what about Petros? Isn't he likely to spring out of the woodwork at any minute?'

He thought she was smiling, but even as she drew slowly closer it was difficult to be sure. 'That's all right. Petros is away in Cyprus, arranging to bring his mother over for the wedding. And Yanni will be out at one of his meetings for a couple of hours. So we are safe for a little while.'

'Safe?' he echoed.

'Please. It may be the last time. I just felt that I would see you again. I felt you had to come, and I was waiting. Nothing else made any sense.'

'Neither does this.'

She was close against him now. There was still a lingering trace of the flower scent, mingled with the hot smell of his bike and the different warmth of Ariadne. 'It's the only thing that *does*. Nick, the other day, you told me you keep thinking about it.'

'I said I did think about it, yes, but – '

'What if I were to call if off? Tell Petros it was all a mistake, and I am coming to you instead. What would you say?' She was in his arms, a blaze of desire. 'What can I do to convince you? You would sooner run away – sooner ride your motor-bike than ride me?' Her hands and hips were insistent. 'You can bear to let me go to another man? *Can* you?'

He parked the bike in the corner of the station yard, alongside the hearse that Billy had acquired, more for its suitability as a passion wagon than an everyday means of transport. It was impossible not to envy Billy. Easy come, easy go: what age would the lad have to reach before he learned the dangers of easy come, difficult to shake off?

'Morning, guv.'

'Morning.'

He was aware of three heads turning to watch him on the way upstairs. He knew what their minds were working on. He had been like them for long enough before promotion. You tried to assess the boss each morning: what mood he was in, what sort of a night he might have had – booze, blondes, dreamless sleep, or a spell of bloody-mindedness.

'Morning, Nick.'

'Morning,' he said automatically as the Red Watch officer came out, ready to hand over.

A couple of official-looking envelopes were waiting on his desk. He opened the top one with some trepidation. You never knew what tinder was in these communications, ready to strike a spark and start a conflagration, maybe with that resurrected menace, D.O. Scase, working hard at the bellows.

It turned out to be a bunch of forms for his application for promotion. They were best kept out of sight until he had the time to work his way through them and decide just what homework he would have to concentrate on.

The second one was routine stuff, but it would give him a chance to flush one little rumour out into the open. He called John Hallam in.

'There's a chore for you, a fortnight from now. A training session.'

'Training? After all these years, guv? I mean . . . '

'Just to broaden your horizons. Temporary assignment to the river police. A fortnight from now,' he repeated, waiting for his sub officer's reaction. When Hallam shifted from one foot to the other without saying anything, Nick added: 'No problems?'

'Er . . . no, guv.'

'I mean, you will be here? Still available?'

If it had been possible for John Hallam's broad, guileless features to look shifty, they would have looked shifty now. He fumbled for words, and at last came out with: 'Why shouldn't I be available?'

'That's what I'm waiting for you to tell me.'

'You've been hearing something.'

'There are some terrible echoes in this place.'

'All right. I've been offered another job. Out of the Brigade altogether.'

'Uh-huh. And that's what you want?'

'Well, it's what Sandra's wanted for a long time. And the more I thought about it, the more it seemed to make good sense.'

Nick thought that he had heard more than enough about good sense recently; though little of it had made any real sense at all. He said: 'So when are you going?'

'I'm not.'

'Glad to hear it. You belong here.'

'But guv – you've known I was up for this, haven't you? You've said as much. So who told you?'

'Like I said, there are quite some echoes in this place, and the walls do seem to have sharp ears.'

'Geoff Pearce,' said Hallam. 'It has to be. Once or twice when I've been on the phone I've thought he was earwigging outside the door.'

'I'm sure he was. But he didn't say a word to me.'

'Then who did?'

'You've heard about keeping mum. There's some wives who wouldn't know the meaning of the word. Especially one heavily disguised as Mrs Pearce.'

'Patti? Oh, Gawd. She didn't hang about, did she? Now I suppose she's going to tell Sandra I turned it down, the moment she gets the chance.'

Nick began to wonder whether his own troubles were really as threatening as those of married members of the Watch. 'You mean you haven't told Sandra yet?'

'It's been a bit tricky, really,' said Hallam

sheepishly. 'She was very keen. She's not going to be very happy about it.'

'Do you suppose Pearce's antennae have picked up your rejection of the offer? Because if Pearce knows, Patti knows for sure. Sounds like a tangled web to me.'

The bells went down.

Billy was tearing the slip from the printer. 'R.T.A. Nelson Road.'

Even Scase could hardly have grumbled at the speed of their turnout.

Sam Brody's wife had been showing him how to use the washing machine – 'And don't put that red shirt of yours in, the colour runs, I always do it by hand' – and scribbling a list of the food in different drawers of the freezer when her labour pains began in earnest. She stopped in mid-sentence, gasped, and inhaled a long, shuddering breath.

'Sam – we'd better go.'

'But I thought they said you'd be about ready to go in this evening.'

'You'd better get me there now. Fast. Please, Sam.'

He raced upstairs to fetch the bag they had packed ready. It had been checked and re-checked a dozen times, but as he dumped it by the front door he said: 'You're sure there's everything? You've got the lot?'

'Get the car out, Sam. Please.'

He got the car to the kerb, helped her towards it, dashed back for the bag, got into the driver's seat and then realized that the front window was wide open. He tripped and almost went down as he stumbled up the path, let himself in, closed the window, and came out again, panting almost as desperately as his wife.

He was driving too fast as he turned the corner from their side street into the main stream of traffic. Somebody blared a horn at him. He tried to pass a beer delivery lorry but had to swing back as a bus veered out in front of him. He sounded his own horn, and a driver at a standstill in the opposite flow of traffic raised two fingers at him.

Susie let out a howl in the back seat. Sam wound his window down just as a camper which had been sitting on his tail made an aggressive move out into the middle of the road. The traffic lights at the crossroads had turned red, and the driver aimed to force his way beside the delivery lorry and take advantage of space behind the oncoming traffic as it cleared the junction.

Sam edged out at an angle to block the way, and leaned out of his window. 'Get back, you stupid – '

'Where the hell d'you think you're going?'

'It's an emergency.'

He was still stuck when the lights turned green. Ramming his foot down, he swung out in a tight arc. At the same time a truck made a last-second dash across the junction, while the camper was trying to cut Sam out. The truck smacked into Sam's bonnet, and the camper bounced off the tangle of two vehicles to crash into one of the traffic light standards.

Sam's head went down sickeningly on to the steering wheel, which had come up to meet him. Susie began to scream, groping for the door handle. It was stuck; and the whole of one side of the car was twisted, while the other was jammed against the high side of the lorry. A stench of spilt petrol began to seep in through a splintered window.

As the appliances slowed down to find a way through the lines of vehicles whose drivers were conscientiously trying to edge up on to the pavement to make room for them, while at the same time cursing their luck in being in this spot at this time, Nick Georgiadis sprang from the cab to push his way through pedestrians and appraise the scene. On the whole, the pedestrians were more obstructive than the car drivers. Dozens had stopped to gape; and were only too eager to offer advice to the station officer.

'There's people in that camper there . . . and fuel all over the place . . . You want to do something about that fuel before you – '

'Just stand back, sir,' said Nick as patiently as he could manage, 'and we'll deal with it.' As the pump found a breach in the traffic, he began deploying his troops. 'Geoffrey, Billy – check on that tailgate. But don't move anything till you're sure you've got it propped up, right? John – have a look at that driver, see if he needs first aid. Kevin, Recall – we need sand on all this fuel round here. What about casualties in that car behind?'

John Hallam had already squeezed through the narrow gap between the camper and the mangled car. The difficulties were immediately obvious. A hysterical young woman was screaming and hammering on the window of a hopelessly warped door. Her husband was slumped over the wheel, bleeding slowly from his left temple. Blue Watch would either have to cut away the whole roof of the car – which would be tricky, tilted and squashed as it was between two other vehicles – or work on removing at any rate the two doors and windows.

'Start on that rear door.'

The cutters set to work.

After ten minutes which seemed more like a hundred, it was possible to free the rear door enough to enable Pearce and George Green to heave it bodily open a few feet, screeching as it came. There was just sufficient space for someone to squeeze out.

Pearce braced himself against the twisted pillar and reached in with his arm. 'Come on, dear. Grab my hand, and I'll haul you out.'

It was only then that they realized she was not in a state to squeeze through that space. There was no way her swollen stomach was going to make it. Pearce called past George's head: 'John – this lady's pregnant.'

The woman screamed again. 'My baby . . . I've got to get out before . . . before . . .'

'There's an ambulance on its way. If you can just hold on a little while – '

'I don't think I can.'

John Hallam said: 'Geoff, can you get in with her?'

'Just about, I reckon.'

'Then get in, and see if you can lift her – gently. Take the weight, and maybe you and George can ease her up.'

Geoff Pearce clambered over the wreckage and edged his way painfully through the gap into the interior. The woman's sobs and convulsive gasps were unnerving. He propped himself against the slanting seat and got his arm round her. 'You hurt?'

'No. I mean, I don't think so, not in any other way, but I can't . . .' She yelped. 'Please, I've got to get out. My baby . . .'

'Ambulance on its way,' said Pearce again. He was still holding her, and could feel the impact of each contraction as it hit her. 'Hold tight.' They had had only one hour about childbirth emergencies on a course long ago, so he was talking without any real conviction. He was clued-up about forcing the water out of a nearly drowned victim's lungs, and about mouth-to-mouth resuscitation, but wasn't in the market for those right now. 'Keep trying. All right, rest a minute. Slow your breathing. Right – have another go.'

The howl of an ambulance approached, and cut off close at hand. One paramedic leaned in to assess the driver's condition. Another braced himself against the door and peered in at the writhing mother-to-be and Pearce.

'No room for me in there as well. Keep up the good work, mate. Any minute now, I'd say. Right, madam. Oblige our friend, will you? Come on . . .'

Susie Brody obliged. After a last despairing howl she sank back, while Geoff Pearce lifted the baby clear, to add its higher and equally piercing squeal to the noise all round them.

'Nice work,' said the paramedic. 'Very neat. Ease yourself out, mate, and I'll take over.'

A round of applause greeted Pearce as he scrambled clear. 'Well done, Geoff. Fires laid, chimneys swept, babies delivered. No job too small, eh? Give the man a cigar.'

'It's going to look funny on the birth certificate, isn't it?' said Billy. 'Place of birth: underneath a truck.'

Nick Georgiadis went round the edges of the tacky carpet of sand and fuel to congratulate Pearce. It was a tale that would go the rounds and last a long time in the Brigade. But he still couldn't summon up the spontaneous comradely feeling there would have been if any other man on the team had done it.

Kevin Medhurst yawned. He had not been up late gambling – he wanted no more wildlife in his own life – but still he felt tired. Staying with Billy had its problems. Billy was very much a night bird. He seemed to come fully awake around ten o'clock, and was insistent that Kevin should accompany him on hunts for other birds – this time the female of the species. His taste wasn't Kevin's. For Billy, availability was all. Kevin liked to think he was more choosy; though there hadn't been much around to choose from recently.

As he slowed behind a bus and yawned again, he spotted a figure in a loose blue jacket, tight blue jeans, and a black baseball cap. Drawing alongside to confirm his guess who it was, he leaned out. 'Care for a lift?'

Sally Reid cast a suspicious look at the kerb-crawling car. Then a grin took over. 'Since it's you, sure.'

He was acutely conscious of the length of her legs as she slid in beside him.

'Think that walking's good for you?' he ventured. 'Or is your Porsche in dock?'

'The old banger's in dock all right. Pranged by that . . . by someone I know. Been borrowing it, forgetting to return it. Forgetting! And now this.'

'That . . .' Kevin had been on the verge of saying 'that big black bastard?' but realized this was not the most tactful remark. Quickly he changed it to: 'That character who was hanging around waiting for you the other evening?'

'That's him. Eddie.'

'Your boyfriend?'

'Ex-boyfriend,' said Sally emphatically. After a few hundred yards, she said: 'All ways up, it's a pest. Come Sunday I was going to nip over and see my dad.'

'Where's he hang out?'

'Wembley. Makes me feel guilty, asking why I don't move back there. I suppose I could get a transfer.'

'You wouldn't do that?'

She glanced at him, surprised. 'Would it worry you if I did?'

'Well, no, of course not.'

But he found himself thinking that the place would lose something if she were not there. She had a way of grinning unexpectedly – a wide grin that seemed to go on expanding for ever and ever into a marvellous, unaffected smile – that lit the place up.

She was smiling now, as if in spite of the unreliable Eddie the whole world was quite a fun place.

Kevin said: 'In spite of everything, you're looking pleased with yourself.'

'Well . . .'

'Come on, out with it. Won the pools?'

'No. But I've won a place on the Brigade swimming team.'

'You never said.'

'I don't tell you guys everything.'

'But you should. It's something to boast about.'

'When I've won a contest, maybe.'

'And when do they have these contests?'

'There's one next Wednesday.'

'Could I come along?'

She was staring straight ahead, her profile dark and remote under the black peak of her cap. But a smile was already simmering again. 'Would you really want to?'

'Yes. Give you some moral support.'

'Any sort of support you get from Blackwall,' she grimaced, 'isn't usually moral.'

The Greek church was tucked between a public garden and a shopping arcade which had gone steadily downhill since the opening of the supermarket. It was not the likeliest rendezvous. Nick hesitated on the steps, wondering why he had been stupid enough to come, and whether he could still walk away and pretend nothing had happened – and take damn good care nothing else did happen from now on.

He went in.

She was sitting in a pew close to the front. His

footsteps resounded in the empty nave, but she did not look round until he had settled beside her. The day after tomorrow the place would be far from empty: she would be here in her wedding dress, and there would be morning suits and floral hats and the rhythmic intonations of the ceremony.

'Why here, of all places?' he demanded.

'I thought it would concentrate our minds on the matter in hand.'

'Why?'

'Petros is back,' said Ariadne. 'He's been asking about you.'

'Oh. What did he want to know?'

'If we'd ever been . . . romantically attached.'

'And?'

Her aquiline profile lifted to contemplate some heavenly distance. She might have been modelling a statue of some virginal, sublime saint. 'It dawned on me,' she said tensely, 'that if I just told him everything, that would be it. He'd go back to Cyprus. Like I said the other evening, I could tell him straight out, and that would be that, and we'd be free to do what we wanted.'

'Apart from the fact that I'd be lynched.' She looked so proud and determined that he had to ask: 'You didn't actually say anything?'

She shook her head. 'But I could do. It's up to you, isn't it?' When he refused to reply, she went on desperately: 'Look, I could just tell them – tell all the family – that it would be impossible for me to marry Petros after what's happened between *us*.'

Sooner or later he had to answer the challenge seething in her dark olive eyes. 'What happened between us the other evening was wonderful,' he said. 'Just great. But it was . . . look, if you want to get out of this marriage just because – '

'I'm prepared to do it if – '

'If what?'

'If you're prepared to make a commitment. What else do you think I'm talking about?'

She waited a long time. Then the sombre pools of her eyes swallowed up the last flicker of her hopeful plea. She got up, pushed her slim legs past his knees, and went back along the aisle.

He followed her to the door. Every word he said seemed cowardly and rotten. But she had known his feelings way back – feelings for her, and feelings against just the sort of commitment she had been pleading for – and he couldn't suddenly abandon everything and surrender.

'This is insane. It's not for me to decide whether you go through with this marriage.'

'Why not? Make a decision for once in your life. Follow your emotions instead of the Brigade rule book. You were impetuous enough the other day.'

'*I* was impetuous? You're the one who's engaged.'

'I don't need reminding.'

'Look, you know how you can make me feel. The effect you have on me. If you want to call off the wedding, that's great. I'd be happy for you. But it's got to be your decision, not mine.'

'Thanks,' she whispered. 'Thanks a lot. Sorry if I've troubled you.'

She sounded as if she hated him so much that it would be a relief to have the whole thing ended once and for all. She went stumbling down the steps, and the clatter of her heels speeded up as she went down the path and along the pavement, until the sound was lost in the clamour of the outside world.

6

That oddly breathy, insinuating voice was murmuring close to her ear before she had sensed anyone coming up behind her. 'Goodness, are you stocking up for a siege?' Patti Pearce, at the end of one of the supermarket aisles, was candidly appraising the contents of Sandra Hallam's trolley.

Sandra very nearly blurted out that it was for tea this afternoon, when three of the other Blue Watch wives were coming round for a natter, but stopped herself in time. The presence of Patti would undermine any free and easy conversation. Patti the Piranha: it wasn't only the Blue Watch men who acquired nicknames.

She said: 'Oh, you know how you run out of everything at once. Have to spend a fortune these days, replacing it all.'

'Anyway, you're obviously not putting John on bread and water.'

'What are you talking about?'

'Oh, come on. After he turned down a job like that? I said to Geoffrey, I said, Sandra had her heart set on him taking that job. I mean, when you gave me a hint last week, I could tell. You did, didn't you?' Patti's eyelids drooped in an unconvincing display of resignation. 'So did I, in a way. After all, what it would have meant to Geoffrey . . .'

Sandra leaned on her trolley. 'Could you run that by me just once more? Because I don't believe I'm hearing this.'

She reached home in a slow, steaming fury. She was only half concentrating as Laura Mackenzie, first to arrive, explained that she would have to leave early to collect Jamie, who was allowed two afternoons a week, if not too tiring, at play school. And she wanted to be sure of being home when Ben got back – *if* he got back. And if he didn't, she dreaded to think what Recall would say when he came off watch. Just when the operation had at last been successfully achieved and Jamie was making such good progress, it was the turn of Ben to raise problems. Made you wonder why you ever bothered to have kids.

'We never had any idea until one of his masters came round to see us,' Laura lamented. 'Tim James. A nice lad, but not much of a disciplinarian. Not like the sort we had in Paisley when I was a girl.'

They had compared notes, and Laura was horrified to find that when Ben left home in the morning he had hardly ever shown up at school. When he did appear, he had said that his mother had kept him at home to help her. The headmaster had ordered the young form master to check with the Mackenzies. Sometimes Ben had stayed at home, telling his mother that he had a whole afternoon of free periods. 'Free periods here and there, yes,' agreed Tim James. 'But they're supposed to do revision in them. And certainly there aren't any afternoons or whole days.' So where had Ben got to when he was neither at home nor in school?

'Skiving.' Sandra felt she had to make some response to Laura's tale of woe. 'Found some undesirable mates, probably. Think they're terribly smart, dodging lessons and mooching round the town.'

'Tearaways.' Laura nodded wretchedly.

'I shouldn't worry, love. He'll soon get bored.'

'He won't have any chance of getting bored.' Laura was suddenly fierce. 'We're not wearing any more nonsense. Lying to me, lying to the school – his dad wasn't going to stand for that. And when Ben said it didn't really matter, he wasn't missing anything, I thought Stuart was going to give him a real going over. And I half wanted him to – and half hated the idea.'

Laura sighed out a sort of laugh, and all at once insisted on helping with the sandwiches. She had got it off her chest, and felt better for it. Sandra felt her own grievances bubbling up inside her, getting perilously close to boiling point. It was time she, too, had a sympathetic audience.

'Well, at least you've got a supportive husband,' she began. 'Unlike some. When I think – '

She was interrupted by the chime of the doorbell.

Jean Quigley made a dramatic entrance. Some years as leading lady in the local dramatic and operatic society had made her prone to sketch histrionic gestures in mid-air with her arms, and mark her entrances and exits with pungent, forceful lines.

Before the front door had closed she declaimed: 'I've left Bert.'

'Oh, not again!' said Sandra automatically.

The Hallams had given Jean sanctuary for more than a week last time, and Sandra was in no mood to suffer all her emotional outbursts again. But she summoned up a shake of the head in commiseration, and led Jean into the kitchen.

Laura glanced round from arranging sandwiches on a tray. 'Hello, Jean.'

Jean put her left hand up to her throat. 'I've had enough.' For a woman fleeing from domestic oppression she looked in good fettle. She had always had a fine, high colour in her cheeks, seeming to reflect the bronze hues in her hair; and the flush of emotion made her boldly etched features even more striking than usual.

Just as she was obviously preparing for her big speech, the doorbell rang again. Sandra gave Clare Wilson an effusive welcome. Her arrival meant they could all hear the tragic tale at once, instead of having it repeated for any newcomer. The second performance might be less compelling than the first.

'I've been a fool,' declared Jean at a volume worthy of a Shakespearean duke as the curtain went up. 'I made a terrible error, persuading him to join that drama group.' Having attended one or two of the company's productions, Sandra silently agreed with her. 'It was just throwing temptation in his way. And he's too feeble to resist it. There was all that trouble last year. And now it's this seedy little blonde who thinks she's the next Emma Thompson. Pathetic. More like one of the witches from *Macbeth*, really.'

Clare looked puzzled. 'But I thought things were going great. Mike said only a couple of weeks ago that Sicknote . . . Bert . . . was having his leg pulled about going off on a second honeymoon.'

'Oh, yes. Quite a leg-pull, that was.'

'It never happened?'

'Depends what you mean by "happened". We went away all right. Romantic weekend in plushy hotel. Only the romance failed to materialize. He preferred to play golf.'

'I didn't know Bert was a golfer.'

'He's not. But he fell in with some loud-mouthed drunk who persuaded him to try a round, and then Bert got hooked on the idea that he was a born champion. What had been meant as a passionate rebirth of love' – Jean stared with tragic intensity into infinity, or at any rate into the far corner of the ceiling – 'turned into me sitting around reading house-and-garden magazines while *he* chased a ball around the countryside or dropped off with exhaustion . . . and snored. And since we've been back, I send him out for a loaf and what does he come back with? A set of secondhand golf clubs.'

'Keeps him out of mischief, anyway,' said Laura unwisely.

'But it hasn't kept him out of mischief. I should have realized something was up when he started playing with the bathroom mirror and his portable shaving mirror to squint at his bald patch.' Jean's derisive snarl was transforming her into Bette Davis. 'He's lamenting his lost youth.'

'Oh, that's a bad sign,' Sandra agreed.

'Then he got that funny smell. Rubbing some foul sort of hair restorer into his scalp – only he came out in a rash! So I said I'd make some porridge.'

'How would that help?'

'When it had set, he could use it as a hair-piece.' Jean began to laugh, then repressed it. She was more at home with melodrama than comedy. 'It has to be something to do with that woman. I ought to have guessed. And then last night I went into the dressing-room and . . .' She paused, staring at each of them in turn. 'And there she was, clinging to him. *Glued* to him.'

'You're quite sure,' said Laura cautiously, 'that it was Bert who made the advances? I mean – '

'Oh, I don't suppose he did. He's not the macho sort. But he certainly wasn't fighting her off.'

'Does he know that you've walked out?'

'Not yet. He'll find out soon enough, when he comes off watch. I've left him a note. And that's all I've left him.'

The other three glanced at one another conspiratorially. The moment any opportunity presented itself, they must coax Jean into returning and tearing up her note. Otherwise they would all suffer a few weeks of miserable monologues and declamations, just like last time.

Laura said: 'Oh, men are impossible. But if it's not one thing, it's another. You just have to look the other way and let it blow over.'

'It's not the one thing that worries me, it's the other. And I'm not going to look the other way.'

Clare said: 'Life at Blackwall does cause a lot of stress, doesn't it? They all have different ways of doing stupid things on and off duty. Sort of compensation, I suppose.'

'Compensation!' Jean scoffed.

'Well, Mike, for one, has been going through a bad patch recently. Only five years to go to his pension, but he's been grouchy with the children, tells me he nearly took a swing at some firefighter in White Watch because of some joke about pranging an appliance – and keeps talking about packing it all in. Maybe we can do it now, since we . . .' She stopped, and glanced at Sandra. 'I think he envies John. Any idea when *he'll* be leaving Blackwall?'

'Never, as far as I can see.'

'But we thought . . .'

It was a cue Sandra was glad to pick up. It was her turn to dominate the stage. And she could handle things just as dramatically as Jean. 'What made you think anything?'

'Well, you know the Brigade. Always some buzz going the rounds.'

'Buzzes, yes. Like a lot of bluebottles round every cranny in the station, looking for something to settle on.'

'So there's nothing in it? Mike thought it might have been Geoff Pearce who overheard something in the first place, and then – '

'Oh, I'll believe that. And then passing it on to that woman. See how far you can get it to go. And how much of a disturbance you can create.'

'But anyway,' said Clare mildly, 'there seemed to be a general feeling that it was all settled.'

'Settled? Do you know exactly how it's been settled? And how I found out?'

She told them the full story. They shifted awkwardly and occasionally looked round at the window as if the predatory face of Patti Pearson might appear there at any moment to create further upsets. When Sandra had finished, there was an uneasy silence.

Laura broke it. 'Clare, what were you going to say about Mike maybe being able to get out?'

'Oh, nothing's settled. Just that we've come into a bit of money. We're thinking about things.'

'Enough to retire on? Some people have all the luck.'

'Oh, no, not that much. Mike thinks there's enough to tide us over until he gets to the pensions and retirement insurance stage. We haven't gone into it in any detail so far.' She drew in her lips slightly. 'So long as there's enough left for the kids.'

'What was it? The pools? National Lottery?'

'My mother-in-law. David's mother. We had a solicitor's letter about going to the reading of her will. I thought maybe she'd left a couple of family mementoes to the boys. A photograph album with pictures of their father when he was little, or something. Never expected there'd be much money there, but she'd piled up quite a little nest egg – split between David's cousin and me.'

Sandra felt enviously that her husband ought to be more like Clare's: Bayleaf actually *wanted* to find a means of getting out, instead of meekly opting to stay.

Laura began to collect her coat and shopping bag. 'Must be off. Got to pick up Jamie – and make sure Ben hasn't gone walkabout again.'

Clare stayed on another half-hour, sitting well back on the couch with that equable smile of hers, while Sandra and Jean competed in the contest as to which of them had been the more shabbily betrayed.

Finally Clare said: 'Time I went, too. I've got the boys to collect from the chess club, and Mike does like me to be in when he gets back.'

'Hm,' grunted Jean.

'And we've got a lot to talk about,' said Clare defensively.

'Hm.'

Sandra accepted wearily that she would have to offer Jean a bed at any rate for a couple of nights while she sorted things out. She cleared the side table while Jean cranked up a further burst of invective against 'that blotchy little tart'. At five-forty, rather than listen to any more of Jean's woes, she turned on the television for the I.T.V. early evening news.

The two of them were only half attending to the succession of politicians pronouncing on crime, educational shortcomings, and the patriotism of highly-paid utilities executives, when a familiar face went swiftly across the screen. It was the Blue Watch station officer. Behind him a house at the end of a block was gushing flame from every window; while down a ladder attached to the roof ridge a firefighter was precariously guiding a woman and baby to another ladder swung in against the guttering. The commentator was describing how the fire had broken out earlier this afternoon, with no explanation of the possible cause so far. A young woman and child had been trapped in an attic bedroom as the fire spread below them. It had been necessary to get them out and then up and over the ridge, and here was the newsreel footage of the final stages: step by step the firefighter backed down, somehow supporting the mother with the baby in a sling round her neck, at the same time guiding his own feet, one after the other on to each rung with agonizing slowness.

There were cheers in the background. A camera cut in quickly to the woman's face. Then it picked up the firefighter, reeling backwards and wiping a hand across his smeared face.

Jean let out a thin little moan. 'It's Bert.'

Sicknote was trying to grin self-deprecatingly at the camera; but on the soundtrack there was the hint of a choking crackle in his throat.

Sandra made a move to put her arm round Jean's shoulders, but Jean was already on her feet. 'I'd better get home right away. He'll need a drink. And something to eat. I might just get there before he gets back.'

One thing Sandra could guarantee: she would be ready and waiting for John when he got back.

She had thought of leading up to it slowly and cannily, feinting and hinting until he began to wonder just how much she knew; getting him on the wrong foot before he summoned up the courage to tell her what he sooner or later had to tell her. But when the time came, she could not hold back. He was no sooner inside the door than she let fly.

'So. You're going to stick with your fire engines, are you?'

'Sandra, just a mo. Wait till I get my – '

'I've waited too flaming long. Waited for you to make something of yourself. And now here we are, back to square one.'

'I don't know what you've heard – '

'You know damn well what I've heard. Not that you had the guts to tell me yourself. Back to dear old Blackwall, eh? You think more of that uniform than you do of me. Or anything else in the real world.'

John struggled to get a word in. 'Look, I said no to a boring job, that's all. I'm a firefighter, for God's sake, not some sort of battery hen. I don't want to spend the rest of my life shuffling bits of paper and answering the phone. You can see that, can't you?'

'What are you asking me now for? You didn't have the decency to consult me before you threw away a good job. I had to find out from Patti the Piranha while I was out shopping. I'm the last person in London to find out anything about you and what you're up to. How d'you think that made me look?'

'If you hadn't gossiped to her about it in the first place, she wouldn't have known anything anyway, would she? First thing she did was go and tell the guv'nor. How d'you think that made *me* look?'

'You don't care what I want, do you? You throw away the best chance we've had in years and you don't even tell me when you do it. It's got to be the guv'nor first, and what the guv'nor thinks of you. You're not married to me. You're married to the bloody Brigade. Well, you can stick with them. I don't have to.' She stormed towards the staircase.

'Look,' John attempted. 'I'd been thinking we might nip down the pub tonight. Sit in a corner and have a chat about things.'

'You've left that a bit late, haven't you?' Sandra paused on the lowest step. 'D'you know what I'm going to do tomorrow? I'll tell you, and you'll be the first to know. Unlike me. I'll tell you. First thing tomorrow I'm going down the labour exchange.'

'What on earth for?'

'To look for a job, of course. Isn't that what they're there for? If you won't change things round here, then I will.'

'What kind of job?'

'Oh, I haven't thought yet. Something useful, like you, maybe. With a nice uniform. Like a traffic warden.'

'Traffic warden? Sandra . . .'

She hurried on her way upstairs, eager not to have her defiant exit line spoilt.

7

At first Bayleaf did not recognize the man standing on the doorstep, smiling eagerly as if they were old friends.

'Mike! Good to see you.'

'Er . . .'

He had seen the face once recently, but still he could fit no name to it.

'I just happened to be in the neighbourhood, and realized I was quite close to your address. Thought I'd drop in just to say hello. Keep in touch, you know. Didn't have much time for a chat last time, did we?'

Clare put her head round the sitting-room door. 'Trevor!'

Now Bayleaf remembered: David Grove's cousin, Trevor Grove, who had shared the unexpected legacy from Clare's mother-in-law. He stood aside, and Trevor moved swiftly indoors. By the time Clare had made coffee, he had already commandeered the coffee table to spread out a hand-drawn plan and some photographs, and was fervently explaining his current activities.

'Look, Clare. Sit you down and let me know how this strikes you.'

He allowed no time for interruptions. His enthusiasm bubbled over, and he twisted the plan around, first towards Clare and then towards Bayleaf, then back again with dizzying speed. The sketch was the ground plan of a restaurant, with a bar, a main food area, toilets, and a kitchen through a door at the end. Trevor's finger gave them a conducted tour. Here he planned to open up a picture window on to the veranda, which at the moment was a purely ornamental waste of space. And if he went through this inner wall he could double the kitchen area as well as giving more space for tables – 'Here . . . and here. Plus the roof needs doing, and I want a complete refurbishment.'

'It certainly sounds ambitious, Trevor,' said Clare.

Bayleaf could tell that she was baffled by all this outpouring; and although he found it interesting, he wondered why Trevor had chosen to spread it out before them like this. Probably it was just that he was so keen on his pet project that he simply had to talk to the first people he met.

'As a matter of interest,' ventured Bayleaf, 'just where is this restaurant?'

'Littlehampton, of course. Didn't I tell you? Lovely site just above the town. Rolling Downs, wonderful sea view. Look.' Trevor extracted a colour picture from under the pile. It had been taken on a sunlit day, and the colours came out radiantly. It was all very different from the trim but featureless street outside.

'I wanted to get all the work done while we're closed for the winter,' Trevor went on, 'but, well . . . time's running short.'

'I don't see why,' said Bayleaf. 'There's plenty of time as long as you get started straight away. Builders can't be that slow in Littlehampton.'

Trevor glanced cautiously at Clare. 'It's not a question of time, Mike. I didn't have much capital lying around, so when I heard that I was mentioned in Aunt Ida's will, I sort of banked on that money to finance all this.'

'Well? You got a tidy sum.'

'Sure.' Trevor hesitated, then said meaningly: 'But not quite as much as I was expecting.'

'Really? We were surprised to get as much as we did,' confessed Bayleaf.

They had in fact been surprised to get anything at all. The thirty thousand quid had come out of the blue, and they were still not quite sure how to cope with it.

'Well, that's the thing, you see. Not that I begrudge the money Ida left you, Clare.'

'Glad to hear it.'

'No, not for a minute. I mean, the old dear thought the world of you and the boys, obviously. But you must admit it was unexpected – you not being related to her, not really.'

Clare was beginning to look uneasy. 'Why are you telling us all this, Trevor?'

'Well, since I was driving up this way anyway, like I said, I thought I'd drop in. And I just happened to have the plans in the car, and I started thinking to myself, Clare came into half of that money, maybe she'd like to make an investment.'

'An investment?'

'In the restaurant. That way we get to expand it, and you buy into a rock solid business. I mean, the punters are swarming all over the place in the summer – can't pack 'em all in.'

'I don't think we'd considered investing the money in a business.'

'What else would you do with it? Shut it all up in a building society? They're a bunch of robbers. Besides, this is family, isn't it?'

'Mike?'

Bayleaf had picked up a glossy photograph of the restaurant interior and was scrutinizing it with growing approval. Trevor might have gone a bit over the top in his enthusiasm, but there was no denying that this looked a pretty attractive prospect. 'Mm, I can see the potential.'

'Why not?' Trevor pressed him. 'Now look, why don't you two talk it over? Come down, have a look at the place. You'll never regret it. It's a little goldmine. Tell you what, I'll leave that set of pictures with you. See how you feel.'

After Clare had shown him out, Bayleaf went on fingering through the prints. They presented an attractive vision of a smart modern building, with a backdrop of low cliffs and glints of sun off the sea. They had all the sparkle of ads from a glossy holiday brochure: just the sort to woo the discerning visitor.

Clare said outright: 'Mike, I don't think I want to let Trevor have our money.'

'We wouldn't be giving it to him. We'd be investing it. Anyway, it wouldn't be every penny of it.'

'We don't know him that well.'

'It'd be a business partnership. All properly drawn up. You don't have to be soul-mates.'

'Can't we just have a slap-up holiday and put the rest in the bank for Melanie and the boys?'

'Look, love, this might be our chance to make a break. Get something going for the future . . . Get me out of the Brigade. And out of London.'

'Is that really what you want?'

'Look, it's your money, basically, so if you don't want to put it into this sort of deal, it's up to you.'

'But you do fancy the idea, don't you?' she said gently.

'Why don't we just go and see the place? Can't do any harm.'

She laughed at his eager expression. 'I guess not. Bit of sea air might do us good.'

Nick was not dressed for the occasion and had not meant even to go near the church; but he found himself driving towards it, turning the corner, and pulling up at the gates just as the bride and groom came out. Even from this distance he could see that Ariadne was exquisite: slender and vibrant in a white silken sheath, her white mantilla emphasizing the darkness of her eyes.

Petros beside her looked smug, as well he might. He was making a great show of waving to his friends and relatives as they came out of the church behind him, beckoning them closer, then turning to grin and chatter at somebody else.

A photographer began dodging to and fro. 'Everybody smile, please. Say "Cheese".'

'No,' Yanni, behind the newlyweds, bellowed out. 'Say "Cheers"!'

'Smile, Ariadne.'

Ariadne obeyed; but then looked down the drive, and saw Nick; and her smile froze.

Yanni, too, had seen him. He came down the path in fine humour, prepared to forgive past misgivings now that the knot was tied and Ariadne was safe. 'Nick, you missed the ceremony.'

'Yes, I'm sorry. Problems.'

'That job of yours – always problems, yes? But come in now, come and join us.'

Ariadne was still staring at him as if daring him to approach. 'I need to change,' he said. 'See you at the reception.'

When he arrived at Uncle Dimitri's restaurant the reception was well under way. The low ceiling trapped the heat and the noise. Couples were dancing; six men were sweating as they performed a complicated Greek dance in one corner, threatening to put a table of wine glasses in great peril; cigar smoke drifted into slowly dissolving whorls. Uncle Dimitri shouldered his way through, a glass in one hand and a bottle in the other. 'Champagne, Nick. Good to see you.' Here, too, Nick had been forgiven.

Except by Ariadne.

She had been dancing with her husband, until Yanni pushed his way in and kissed her and took their arms, and the three of them swayed to the metallic twang of the bouzouki music for a few minutes before a friend plucked at Petros's arm and tugged him away. Ariadne turned to come face to face with Nick.

'Congratulations,' he said.

Pride and fury battled in her eyes. 'You satisfied now?'

Before he could answer, Petros was calling: 'Ariadne.'

Nick said quietly: 'Your husband's calling you.'

She flinched, and turned away.

There was no point in staying here. The champagne was tasteless. The noise was overpowering and meaningless. He headed for the door.

A familiar voice said: 'Nick. In a hurry to escape?'

It was Diana – the boss's daughter whom, like Ariadne, he had escaped. And still wasn't quite sure whether either decision had been an especially brilliant one.

'Hello.'

She had that same quizzical, half-mocking look to which he had so often been treated. 'You look as if you need a big drink.'

He was tempted to stay, and talk, and drown out some memories while reviving others. But it wouldn't work: hadn't worked before, wouldn't work now.

'Not really. Sorry, but I've got to go.'

'I'll call you.'

It was disturbing. There were too many echoes. *I'll call you*: just the way Ariadne had said it; and look at the risks that that had led to, and afterwards led nowhere.

He was free from any commitments, and he was going to stay that way.

The sea air that Bayleaf had spoken of came at them long before the Channel itself was visible. Grass on the Downs rustled and quivered in a steady breeze, and through the open window of the car came a tang of ozone. In spite of her reservations, Clare put her head back, breathed long and deep, and looked as if she were beginning to enjoy herself.

Although Trevor had dictated instructions over the phone, at first approach Bayleaf overshot the unmarked side road and had to go some way before he could find a farm entrance in which it was safe to turn. The side road, when he got on to it, did not look the kind to provide a busy passing trade from large convoys of holiday-makers; and the glimpse of sea was rather less spacious than the artful photographs had suggested. But at least The Mill Restaurant was on a high, airy site, and the stump of windmill preserved in the neighbouring field looked suitably historic and romantic.

The only other car in the car park was a Range Rover. On the chipped, lumpy surface, still holding puddles from a recent shower, it looked a more suitable vehicle than Bayleaf's Metro.

As they got out, Clare ran a critical eye along the frontage of the building. Trevor had said the place was thriving. It didn't look very thriving. But then, Bayleaf assured himself, it was out of season.

Trevor came bouncing out of the main entrance, his hand outstretched before he was within twenty yards of them. He wore a smart grey double-breasted suit and a silk tie, and his smile was wide and hospitable.

'Hello, hello. Found it all right, then?'

'Might do better if you had a sign on the corner down there. Let 'em know you're here.'

'Took it down when we closed for renovations, Mike. Goes back up when we're ready to deal with the hungry again. Come and have a look.'

Bayleaf had to admit that it wasn't quite the smart, gleaming place he had envisaged. Tables piled with chairs and pushed back against the walls looked chipped and discoloured. There were thick rivulets of congealed grease across the carpeting. But Trevor's patter was painting a very different picture of what lay beyond the present reality.

'First thing we do is sort the floor space out and get another twenty covers in. I've turned more than that away on a good day. Get the decor a bit more with it, too. Last lot did it out a bit naff. We can do better than this, can't we?'

'Hope so,' murmured Clare.

To counterbalance her quiet doubts, Bayleaf tried to match Trevor's cheerfulness. 'Don't see why not, if the trade's here. Long as the kitchen can cope.'

Trevor took him matily by the arm and led him to a door beside the bar. 'Know what's up there? Service flat. Couple of rooms, little bathroom. Yours if you want to use it. Spend some time here. Save you travelling up and down.'

Bayleaf liked the idea. He looked at Clare, waiting for her to agree.

'Yes,' she said. 'If we could leave the kids.'

He was in no mood to be depressed by minor details. Everything could be sorted out once you got down to it. It would be great to spend half the week here during his off-duty spells. They could get the place up and running, and then when he had packed in the Brigade they could live down here all the time.

'Look,' Trevor was rattling on, 'everything's on paper. Ask my accountant, he'll take you through it. Anything you don't like, just say so. That's fair enough. It's your money going in, as well as mine, right?' Before Clare could express any reservations, he was hurrying them round to the far end of the bar. 'The kitchens. You were mess manager, Mike, you'll know all about this.'

Trevor was not a man to waste any time. Two days after they were back in London, a letter arrived from his accountant. It read very convincingly, brisk and professional. He had been informed of Mr Trevor Grove's proposal to establish with Mr and Mrs Michael Wilson joint management of The Mill House restaurant in Old Mill Lane, near Littlehampton, West Sussex. Papers to this effect could be prepared by Friday next and would be passed to Mr Grove for their mutual signatures. Perhaps Mr and Mrs Wilson would be kind enough to confirm their willingness to proceed.

Clare took a long time reading and re-reading what was only a short letter. Bayleaf could tell that now it was set down in writing, she was having further doubts. Each time they discussed it he was able to coax her round; but then, next day, she would be fretting again. For himself he was ready to squash any doubts. He would hang on to the Brigade for as long as he had to, but he was dying to get this project off the ground: to get something working for them, instead of always working for somebody else while he just went on getting older. This was it, he was sure of it. The money, the offer, everything: it all felt right.

He set about reassuring Clare yet again.

8

There were three of them, all within a matter of ten days. At first no one had any reason to suppose any connection between a woman drowned, a man stepping off a balcony into thin air, and a man apparently bursting spontaneously into flames. Each was a separate incident; until Peter Whale came on the scene.

It began with the woman. Blue Watch was called just after dawn one calm April morning to the lock gates of Blackwall Basin. On the mudbanks flanking the gates, a rotting barge was keeled over against the river wall. It was one of those hulks which everyone in authority and every boatman on the river said ought to have been broken up and shifted long ago; but nobody acknowledged ownership, and nobody would accept the responsibility and the cost. As the tide sank this particular morning, a dock security guard reporting for shift changeover noticed a dark shape wedged between the wreck and the south pier of the dock entrance. If the dawn light had touched it at a slightly different angle he would probably have paid it no attention: it could have been just another shadow in the murk of stained planking and grey mud. As it was, the light picked out what looked like the head of a seal; but seals had not so far been known to make an appearance this far up the Thames, and it did not seem to be moving or making any attempt to swim clear of the trap out into the tideway.

He edged along the side pier and shone his torch down. The face was not that of a seal or any other fish or animal: it was that of a young woman. She must have floated in and been caught between two jagged planks, too firmly wedged to swim free or be carried out by a shift of current.

The river police arrived, but found the body was indeed firmly gripped by the wooden claws. The two river fire tenders on duty were co-operating with Rotherhithe Fire Station duty crew on a waterside timber store blaze. A Blackwall contingent was the nearest available team with the facilities to extract the corpse.

Blue Watch had freed many a drowned or half-drowned person trapped under bridges or crushed against moorings by canal boats. The steepness of the river wall and the depth of the mud made this present chore a bit trickier than most; but it still took only twenty minutes to cut the woodwork away and lift the dead woman on to dry ground.

John Hallam looked sadly down into her face. Some of the waterlogged corpses they had dealt with had been so bloated and disfigured that it was hard to recognize them as human beings – and perhaps best not to try. But this young woman could not have been in the water long: perhaps only since last night. She could have been quite pretty, and there were no signs of pain or struggle on her face. Rather the opposite: she looked quite tranquil, and her pouting lips seemed almost to be smiling. The only mark on her was a slight red graze, creepily like the shape of her lips, on her forehead.

'Must have scraped herself along the hull before she got stuck,' suggested Sally. She, too, looked sad: loving to be in the water, swimming, she could not imagine being betrayed by it, claimed by it.

After three or four days the police had still been unable to identify the corpse. A number of people who had reported a daughter or wife missing came forward to inspect it; but none of them could offer any help.

It was just another incident to be recorded in the Blackwall log and forgotten.

Hallam felt only a faint prickle of curiosity when Station Officer Frank Suffolk of White Watch commented at changeover one morning on the frustration he had felt at losing a jumper. So many of those threatening to throw themselves off balconies or rooftops were really begging to be rescued. They waited to be talked out of it. The danger was always that of the demonstrator growing impatient, or losing his own grip on what he genuinely wanted, and actually making the jump 'just to show 'em'. So in this case a trained interrogator had been rushed in to do the talking, while the crew of the pump ladder approached from the rear of the building. The man had been standing there in a trance, not calling out any histrionic pleas or cursing some faithless girlfriend, which was so often the pattern. To keep things in a low key, the sound of the appliance closing in was muffled by a throb of police vehicles revving up immediately below the balcony of the block of flats.

Listening to Suffolk's story, Hallam remembered Recall getting just such a man from behind while the dialogue went on at the front. White Watch had been less fortunate. The man had been indifferent to pleas from below. He surveyed the streets and houses with a long, reminiscent stare; then, drawing himself up to his full height, he smiled a seraphic smile and stepped contentedly off the edge into space.

'Could have been on drugs, we thought,' said Suffolk irritably. 'But the forensic boys checked, and there was no trace of them. Makes no sense. And even after he'd hit the ground his face was almost unmarked, and the silly sod seemed to be grinning at us as if he'd deliberately taken the mickey out of us. Hardly a mark, except for one graze on his forehead.'

Something just below the surface of Hallam's recent memory stirred. 'Like a mouth – a couple of lips?'

'That's right. How the hell did you know?'

'It's only a coincidence.'

He told Suffolk about the mark on the drowned woman's brow. It had to be a coincidence. There had been plenty of far more dramatic coincidences during their professional careers, and this was a pretty minor one: a scratch on the brow of a woman dragged by the current along the side of a crumbling hulk; a bruise on that of a man falling from a great height.

Then there came the third.

In the middle of a Thursday afternoon the bells summoned the Watch from a spell in the exercise room, calling for attendance at the supermarket.

'Somebody trying out a pack of kitchen matches to make sure they work?' hazarded Billy.

'Or an overheated customer going through the roof.'

There was a grisly truth in that. Two counters were on fire, ignited by a man who had stood in the aisle between them and simply caught fire. That was the story, afterwards, of a supervisor and two girls behind the perfume counter who had seen it start. The man had been standing there – 'just looking at me,' shivered one of the girls, 'as if he could see right through me at something else on the other side, like' – and all at once he had caught alight. One moment he was staring bemusedly into nowhere; the next, he was ablaze, and yet he went on standing there without uttering a sound.

Spontaneous combustion, thought Hallam sceptically. There had been a spell when a lot of magazines and television programmes had researched that, listing scores of well-authenticated stories of people who had spontaneously caught fire and been consumed without apparently feeling any pain.

No examples of this had ever been reported by any fire brigade that John Hallam knew of.

But certainly here a man had been on fire and had come close to setting the entire premises on fire. There was little to be done with the remains of the man himself. The crew doused down the two adjoining counters, to the accompaniment of groans from the supervisor as several yards of stock were systematically ruined, and George Green called for an ambulance to remove the body.

Before it arrived, Hallam bent over the hideously blistered face of the victim.

'Just stood there.' One of the girls was shuddering from belated shock. 'Never made a sound. Just went up in flames, and didn't look as if he could feel a thing.'

There was no question of spontaneous combustion. The tell-tale smell of petrol mingled with the smell of charred flesh and burnt clothing. He must have soaked himself – or been soaked – before coming into the supermarket, and could have struck a match without it being obvious.

'Some political demonstration?' asked a familiar voice above Hallam's head. 'A protest against using animal products in the perfumes?'

Hallam stood up. 'If so, he didn't announce his doctrine before he torched himself.'

It could have been embarrassing, finding Peter Whale right beside him, after turning down that generous offer of a job. But Jonah seemed quite unperturbed.

'What d'you make of it then, old son?'

'Not back in an F.I.U., are you?'

'No. Still in the same place. This firm happens to be one of our more important clients. Security and all that. And they'll want a full report on how someone could damn near set fire to the place without any obvious reason, and without anyone suspecting his movements.'

'You could hardly be expected to foresee a nut case doing a demo on the premises in the middle of the day.'

'How little you know, old lad. Damage to store goods is a matter for deep concern – financial concern – and anguished recriminations. Somebody has to be blamed. They'll want their money's worth. There has to be an explanation somewhere, fed into the computer and printed out in quintuplicate.'

Jonah became aware that Hallam was only half listening, bending back over the man's face. The ambulance would be too late. He was dead. 'Spotted something?'

'More than a spot,' said Hallam. 'A scar – or a burn.'

'In the middle of all that – one burn worth singling out?'

'It's funny, but I think that one little mark was there before the rest of him got burnt.'

'Signifying what?'

As the ambulance arrived and the paramedics shook their heads over the remains they now had to remove, Hallam explained with some diffidence the coincidence of the drowned woman, the man who had stepped out blithely to his death fall, and now this man who had endured self-immolation without, according to witnesses, appearing to suffer any flicker of pain – each marked with that barely noticeable little ellipse on the forehead.

'Stigmata?' mused Jonah. 'Or something self-inflicted?' He grinned suddenly. 'Still doing detective work, John? I knew you were cut out for it. Wasted at Blackwall.'

'Look, Peter, I told you I was sorry to turn that job down, but there's something about the place . . . the station, the whole bloody old building and . . . well . . .'

'You know what Jeremy Taylor said.'

'Remind me.'

'"Our soul is, above half it, earth and stone in its affections and distempers." Homesteads, places. This plot of earth. Earth and, of course, air, fire and water. The basic elements. Hm. I wonder if . . . no, that's a bit farfetched.'

'All right, Peter, I'll buy it. What have you got in mind?'

'Farfetched,' repeated Jonah. 'But I think I'll risk running it up the flagpole for the police and see who salutes it – or shoots it down.'

Quentin Barr had been fearing for many days that the police might show up. At the same time he had an inner conviction that there was nothing to worry about. Whatever happened, his beliefs would prove strong enough to sustain him. His staunch community had the spiritual strength to withstand any assault by the forces of the solid world that would so soon cease to exist. Soon there would be nothing solid on this plane of being. All that was desirable lay beyond. Miriam, Charles and Darrell had gone ahead. They would keep the way open. However viciously the forces of materialism attempted to close in, they could not hope to block the way of those who had the knowledge of true power.

Even so, he felt a quickening of the pulse when he opened the door to a man and woman in everyday clothes but with the grey aura of uniform thinking and limited imagination.

'Mr Barr? Mr Quentin Barr?'

'I am he.'

'Detective Inspector Wainwright and Detective Constable Grant.' They both showed their warrant cards. 'Do you think we might have a word with you, sir?'

'By all means.' Barr stood back to let them in. 'How can I help? There hasn't been another break-in at the tobacconist's?'

'Not that we know of, sir.' The D.I. glanced around the room at the framed diagrams of astrological charts and the statuettes of symbolic figures from a religion beyond his comprehension. 'It's more to do with . . . well' – he gestured at the small altar with ebony candle-holders set against the eastern wall of the room – '*this*.'

'You're interested in transcendental studies, inspector?'

'Only when it might have some bearing on our professional inquiries.'

'Inquiries into what?'

'Three deaths,' said Wainwright, suddenly aggressive.

'I'm afraid I don't understand. I'm not aware of being involved in any deaths.'

'You know a . . .' Wainwright silently consulted his constable, who read from her notebook: 'Mr Brian Howard.'

'I do. Or did. He is no longer with us.'

'He certainly is not. And . . . ?' Again Detective

Constable Grant spoke for him: 'Mr Charles Wilde.'

'Another sad loss.'

'The late Mr Howard's parents,' said Wainwright, 'and the late Mr Wilde's sister have informed us that you had an unhealthy influence on them.'

'Unhealthy?' Barr managed a tolerant laugh.

Wainwright looked around the room again, this time accusingly. 'Filled them with dangerous beliefs which could have led to their deaths.'

'Dangerous? In what way?'

'That's what we'd like to know, Mr Barr. Was there anything in the rituals, or whatever, of your little sect which – '

'We do not carry out rituals, and we are not a little sect. We are part of a vast worldwide community devoted to meditation and preparation for an imminent life to come.'

'Worldwide?' said Wainwright sceptically.

'Let us rather say cosmos-wide.'

'Why should they both have committed suicide? Were they taking drugs?'

'I am sure your experts must have checked on that.'

'Yes, well. Or hypnotized?'

'Thinking people do not necessarily have to be drugged or hypnotized in order to decide that it is time to leave this world for a better one.'

'Both of them,' snapped Wainwright, 'had odd

red marks on their foreheads. Almost like Indian caste marks.'

'In our community there are no castes. No distinctions of class or colour.'

'Look, Mr Barr, what exactly does this sect of yours teach?'

'Not a sect,' Barr corrected him again. 'We call it a community of the elements. A true acceptance of the powers of earth, fire, air and water. We believe in all humility that with the coming of true awareness of the balance, the world as we know it will soon end, and the elements will come together and the catalyst of our belief will fuse them into one, which will be an immortal element beyond our present understanding. If you're genuinely interested, inspector, I'll gladly let you have a copy of our principles, so that you can study them at leisure. We have nothing to hide.'

'And these two deaths have nothing to do with your . . . group? Pure coincidence that the two men should have been members?'

Barr bowed his head reverently. 'Perhaps they were too impatient. One gets some slightly unbalanced, impetuous people in one's community now and then.'

'You can say that again.' Wainwright glanced fretfully at his constable, and tried a last clumsy attack: 'And you wouldn't know anything about a young woman who was drowned ten days ago near Blackwall Basin – with a similar mark on her forehead?'

'What was her name?'

'That,' said Wainwright reluctantly, 'we don't know. Nobody's come forward to identify her. And she doesn't fit the description of any persons reported missing.'

Of course not. Miriam's mother and father were themselves members of the community, and would not have dreamt of reporting Miriam missing or coming forward to identify the mere husk that she had sloughed off. Their only sadness was in the envy they felt for her having gone ahead of them into the beyond.

'I don't seem to have been much help, inspector.'

'No,' said Wainwright. He accepted the booklet Barr was handing him – gingerly, as if it might explode in his hand. 'But perhaps we may have to come back to you, sir. You won't be going away in the near future?'

'No.' It was a lie; but he was not going to tell a creature of such poor comprehension just when and where he would be going.

When the two detectives had left, doubtless to put in a heavily biased and insensitive report about their petty suspicions, Barr closed his eyes and silently apologized to Miriam and Charles in their afterworld, sure that they would forgive him. It had been necessary temporarily to disown them and deny the motives of their self-sacrifice, for the sake of the whole community. They had each taken the symbolic kiss of fire on their brows and made their individual contribution to liberating the psychic strength of the community in preparation for the final immolation which all craved. Now there were only a few days to go, and there must be no delays in the ordained process caused by ignorant police meddling. The pattern must not be disrupted.

At midnight on the eighteenth of April the chosen flock would assemble in the appointed church around the brazier and votive candles to celebrate the trinity of fire, air and water before renouncing the earth and all that was earthly.

The bells went down. Billy came out waving the print-out. 'Fire St Luke's, Tanpits Road.'

'But that's been boarded up these past five years. Time the place was pulled down.'

'Looks like someone's decided to burn it down instead.'

As they approached, one section of the wooden boarding which filled the blank window spaces was ablaze, fanned by a boisterous wind, and another was beginning to buckle. As the hoses were reeled out, a noise that was not just that of the wind or the familiar roar of flames came thinly from inside the derelict church. It was an eerie blend of agonized screaming and monotonous chanting.

'Guv, the west door's open. If they want to get out, why the hell . . .'

Hell was inside. As Sicknote and Recall drove the jets of water ahead of them they might have been pacing into a hideous medieval painting of the floor of hell. Men and women blazed like human torches, some writhing and screaming yet trying in spasms to sing through their agony, some walking hypnotically in and out of the heart of the fire as if immune to pain.

Recall tried to drive two of them into the fine, fierce droplets of the nearest jet. Another twitched into wakefulness, cried out, and lumbered of his own accord towards the door. A man who had been standing in the pulpit, as yet untouched, called: 'No, Simon. In moments we shall be cleansed, and we shall go through.'

He saw Recall advancing on him, and slid down the pulpit steps, dodging round two burning women and making for the flames himself. Hit sidelong by the full force of one of the hoses, he was knocked along the aisle towards the door. Billy grabbed him and thrust him out into the open.

'No, you have no right. I am Quentin Barr, I am their guide and I must lead them. I must be with my people.'

Barr tried to stagger back inside. Billy was in no mood for patient discussion. 'Stupid sod.' He dragged Barr backwards until they collided with the crumbling edge of a table tombstone, and left him sprawled over it while he went back to the doorway, blocking it as he helped Recall steady a leaping, thrashing hose.

Barr struggled to his feet and ran round the side of the doomed church, his gaze fixed on the flames devouring the wooden panels of one window space.

Hallam grabbed him. 'Look, sir, if you want to rescue your friends, you'd best leave it to us. We do know what we're doing.'

There was an ominous tearing of metal above their heads. A long section of guttering came down towards them like a twisted spear. Hallam sprang to one side. Released, Barr made a wild leap up to the sill of the shattered window, and stood with his arms raised as the flames embraced him. Once he looked ecstatically back, and then Hallam saw him no more as he pitched through the crackling, disintegrating wood into the furnace of the interior.

It was crazy. And sickening. Hallam had seen plenty of hideous sights in his years with the Brigade, and had learned to harden himself against the stench of burning flesh. What turned his stomach now was the expression on the face of that man in his nauseating delirium: he had looked almost as if he were enjoying himself in that final conflagration – because somehow he didn't believe it was final.

9

The end was nigh. Reaching the forecourt of the fire station with Billy chattering like a randy budgerigar beside him, Kevin knew that he must move on. Sharing accommodation with Billy had been meant only as a stop-gap. Now it was time to cross the gap and free himself. He couldn't take much more.

'So she didn't come across?' Billy was asking. 'That why you look so frustrated?'

'Why d'you think I got home way ahead of you?'

'Didn't know you had, till this morning. Me, I came home with the milk.'

'The brewer's dray, more like.'

'Well, we had a few drinks, all right. Didn't your bird? I thought she was hard at it when I left you.'

'Oh, sure. Most of it came up again in my car. In

case you didn't notice, I had to get up early to clear it all up so it doesn't stink when I go out tonight.'

'Oh. Going out tonight, are we?'

'No. *I* am.'

'On the prowl, eh? Or going back to give her another chance?'

'Look, do you know what happened when I did finally get her home? Her dad comes to the door and starts yelling blue bloody murder at me.'

'Better luck next time.'

'There won't be a next time.'

A young man dodged across the forecourt towards them, beaming a welcome. His mouth and eyes were craters in a moon-like face, eager to engulf anyone who came near.

'Morning, Billy,' he said affectionately. 'Morning, Kevin.'

'Hello, Donald.' Billy fished out some coins. 'Here, if you wouldn't mind getting the *Mail* for me.'

'Oh, I will, Billy. Count on me. Thanks.' Donald hesitated a moment. 'Going to let me on one of the engines one day?'

'One day.'

Geoffrey Pearce was standing by the door of the appliance bay. 'Who *is* that weirdo?'

'Hark at who's talking,' muttered Billy.

'It's only Donald,' said Kevin hastily. 'No harm in him.'

'He gives me the creeps.'

Billy mouthed something behind Pearce's back. Bayleaf, crossing the forecourt, added: 'A bit simple, that's all. Must be, the way he adores firefighters.'

'Don't let him on the forecourt again.'

'But it's all he lives for.'

'You heard what I said.'

After roll-call, Billy emerged to find the eager Donald waiting patiently with the newspaper under his arm. Unfortunately Pearce had chosen to follow Billy out.

'Look, lad, this won't do. It's not safe. Appliances come out of here at high speed.'

'I know.' Donald beamed his adoration.

'So you'll be better keeping to the far side of the road.' Pearce was spelling it out syllable by syllable, very loudly.

'I won't get in the way, honest. I never do.'

'The other side of the road,' Pearce grated.

Donald cowered like a dog shrinking from a hostile tone of voice, and slunk away.

Kevin found that Sally was beside him, sharing his contempt for Pearce's attitude. 'All set for this evening?'

'I told you, don't spread it abroad.' She sounded oddly on edge.

The smell of chlorine wafted up from the indoor pool to the balcony, where supporters of the different contestants were keeping up a babble of good-natured joshing which boomed back off the tiles and the roof. Kevin recognized a few faces: a couple of men from Green Watch, and a woman sub from Rotherhithe. There was no one but himself from Blackwall Blue Watch. Sally had been adamant about keeping this evening's race a secret.

She had been very quiet in the car on the way here. He put it down to nerves, but didn't want to unsettle her with meaningless encouragement. Only when she went off to the changing cubicles did he say: 'You'll make it. You can't fail – just think of my moral support, holding you up in the water.' She rewarded him with a faint grin, and he was sure that once she got going she would give it all she'd got.

An echoing announcement jangled round the building. Kevin leaned forward on the rail and looked down as the competitors came out. Sally's dark brown figure in her snugly fitting costume was quite a revelation. Until now he had seen her only in firefighter's gear or casual everyday clothes. This evening she was stripped down to reveal a lithe beauty and strength – she would never have made it into the Brigade without that physical fitness – but there was no suggestion of the tough sinews or meatiness of the professional athlete.

She went gracefully into the water at high speed, and at once was pulling ahead of her rivals. Supporters were yelling, urging their contenders on, even though the swimmers could almost certainly hear nothing. Kevin cheered; cheered again as she made a swift turn at the end of the pool; then groaned to himself. Sally was flagging. The terrific impetus slackened. Her arms went on driving her through the water, but first one rival and then another overtook her. She managed to come in third by just a few inches. For a moment she sat on the edge of the pool with her head down, taking in despairing gulps of air; then got shakily to her feet and padded slowly away, still with her head down, to change.

When Kevin met her outside, all the fervour had gone out of her. He touched her arm, but she was rigid and unyielding.

'Come on.' He steered her towards the car. 'You just weren't on form for once.'

'No. I wasn't. I ought to have known.'

'How could you have known? I mean –'

'Eddie,' she suddenly exploded. 'Bloody Eddie again.'

'He hasn't been round again?'

'No. But the police have. Shoved their way into my flat last night. Looking for him – or anything he might have left behind. They turned the place inside out, chucked everything around, and then cleared off without as much as a "Sorry to have troubled you." Treated me like dirt.'

When they stopped outside the block of flats, she appeared too weary to get out of the car. He said:

'Look, you were thrown. Nothing to do with the way you swim when you're in the mood. Anyway, it was only a race. There'll be plenty more. You win some, you lose some. I should know – I'm a card player.'

'Yeah, only a race. And me with a losing hand.' At last she heaved herself out on to the pavement. 'Come in for a minute, will you? Have a coffee. I don't fancy being on my own right now.'

Indoors, she sniffed. 'The place smells. Contaminated. I feel as if I've been burgled. Walked all over with dirty feet.'

There was a crack in her voice. He put an arm round her shoulder. It moved in a slow, grateful response. He kissed her. She murmured, tried to move away, but instead let her head sink against his shoulder.

'Forget about it,' he said. 'And now, what about that coffee?'

'Coffee?' She moved her head away an inch, then let it sink back again. 'Let's forget about that, too.'

D.O. Scase arrived, as before, without any warning, acknowledged the hasty welcome of Leading Firefighter Pearce with a brief grunt, and made his way straight upstairs to the station officer.

'Just a routine check, Georgiadis. Can I have a look at your attendance records?'

Nick pulled open the top drawer in the cabinet.

As he turned back towards the desk he saw Scase staring down at the Form 1721 there.

'Chasing promotion, are we?'

Without a word Nick laid the register on top of the application form. Scase ran his gaze down the open page with the malevolence of a disgruntled schoolmaster confident of spotting a misspelling.

He was not disappointed. Nick could feel the little jerk of triumph, and there was an added rasp in Scase's voice as he said: 'Firefighter Wilson seems to have been in two places at once.'

'May I see, sir?'

Scase's forefinger jabbed down twice. Unhappily it was true: the sickness log had Bayleaf down for leave on the twenty-third of last month, but on that date he was also marked as present. The D.O.'s morning had been made, and he was ready to be on his way. 'I'll leave you to deal with that. But you know, Georgiadis, I've visited this station several times in recent weeks, and I have to say that each time I've been disturbed by what I've found. Blackwall,' he admonished, 'has more to live up to than most. It was narrowly saved from closure not long ago. I'd hate to think the efforts of A.C.O. Bulstrode were misplaced.'

'With respect, sir' – Nick kept his voice steady with an effort – 'you found one minor error.'

'The tip of a very large iceberg, I fear.' Having enjoyed himself, Scase attempted a soapy smile. 'Would you like me to take your application back with me to Lewisham? Wouldn't want it to arrive late, the posts being in their present parlous state.'

'Thank you, sir, but I think I'll take it myself.'

'No doubt you'll be dropping in to see A.C.O. Bulstrode while you're there.'

'Why? He hasn't sent for me.'

'As I understand it, you're a friend of the family.'

So that was what he understood, was it? It would have given Nick some pleasure to tell him that he was way behind the times; but not enough pleasure to be worth the risk of irritating the little parasite even further.

When Scase had gone, he summoned Hallam in and confronted him with the discrepancy.

'Sorry, guv. Must have been my fault. It was when Bayleaf was off two days, getting over that bash on the head. I just automatically put him down as being present. Sorry.'

Nick sighed. 'I warn you. Scase hasn't finished with us yet. He'll be back for more. He intends me to suffer for the sins of my predecessor.'

'It wasn't Mr Tate's sins, guv. Scase was the one who got it all wrong.'

'Which only makes him all the more venomous.' Nick noticed that Hallam, too, was taking a look at the 1721 application form on the desk. 'Right, what about that fire precautions inspection at the Gourmet Gondola, or whatever it calls itself nowadays? Time they had a surprise visit.'

'I'll take Sicknote and Bayleaf. And Billy.'

'Keep Billy away from the waitresses. We don't want Scase to add sexual harassment to our misdeeds.'

Kevin was in the watchroom as the appliance slid out at less than its usual speed, and without any blues and two-tones. He saw Sally watching it go; and as she turned back into the bay, he leaned out and said: 'Called you this morning. Thought we could have met up.'

'So where were you?'

'Trying to get away from Billy. Me and my watchdog!'

'You haven't said anything to him – I mean, about . . . ?'

'Course I haven't. But he's got a very sensitive nose.'

'Nosey, yes. But sensitive?'

'He knows what time I go out, and what time I get back at night. Or not get back.'

'Guard dog, watchdog – quite a handful.'

'I'm getting out. Paid a month's rent on a houseboat today on the canal. That's why I called you.'

'Good for you. But you don't need my approval to get Billy out of your life.'

'I just wanted you to have a look, see what you thought.'

'About what?'

He had expected her to get the drift by now. 'See whether you like it or not. I mean, I can manage there on my own, but . . . well, it's big enough for two, and . . . well . . .'

She got the message this time. For a moment her full lips seemed to tighten in anger. Then she smiled faintly; but it was not an oncoming smile. 'I don't think so, Kev. Not quite the best idea of the year.'

'If you're not doing anything tomorrow afternoon,' he persevered, 'come and have a look. You can always go home again.'

'And what if I didn't? We know what would happen, don't we? And then what would we do – come back on duty at six o'clock, arm in arm?'

10

John Hallam arrived home to find his wife smartly done up in a new, sleek brown woollen dress, very figure-hugging. Also she was wearing the dangly earrings he had bought her for Christmas.

'Well?' she demanded.

He felt a moment's panic. 'Are we due somewhere? I'm not late?"

'Oh, Lor'. You never remember a thing, do you?'

Now it came back to him. Her evening classes in computers and office management. 'You look great,' he said hurriedly.

'Whizzkid in the making? Senior secretary?'

'Given time.'

'Honestly!' She kissed him and turned towards the door. As she reached it he realized how very special she did look. Years of marriage hadn't done much damage to her figure. It was just that he didn't often notice it. Now she was dressed in a way that would make other people notice.

He said: 'Hey, this is only an evening class. You're not trying to impress the chairman of I.C.I. or something.'

'May as well begin the way I mean to go on.'

As she was reaching for her brief-case, the phone rang. Sandra picked it up, listened and made a mocking face, and said: 'That was Patti.'

'Didn't know you were buddies.'

'We're not. But the way she puts it, they're only just round the corner, and she needs a man.'

'Eh?'

'She wondered if you could go round and fix her electrics. She's in the dark. All the lights have gone off.'

'What about Geoffrey?'

'He's gone out.'

'Well, can't she wait until he gets back?'

'She says she can smell burning. You know how much you enjoy that sort of thing.'

He had been looking forward to sinking into a chair and drowsing over the evening paper once she had gone. 'Those bloody Pearces. Never know what they'll be scrounging round for next. We should never have let them come to live so close.'

'How exactly could we have stopped them?'

Grumbling as he shrugged his coat on and took a large torch from the hall cupboard, he followed her out. Under the street lamp he took another look at her. 'Sandra, you do look great. Great.'

She smiled a gorgeous smile.

He trudged off along the road and into the crescent, wondering to himself where Geoff Pearce had got to: he wasn't the sort to frequent pubs and make pals in the local, and there were no clubs in the neighbourhood that he'd be likely to join – or that would have him. Solitary, meditative walks?

Patti greeted him with a warm whisper, closing the door so quickly behind him that she brushed against him and almost lost her balance. 'It's so lovely of you to come.'

'Where's the fusebox?'

Her hand closed over his. 'I'll steer you there. Mind the edge of the heater. All right . . . John?'

The fault took only a minute to locate. 'Not a fuse,' he explained as the lights came on. 'Just that the trip had gone. Probably something temporary. But if it does it again, you'd better have a thorough check.'

'Many a trip twixt the cup and the lip, eh?' Patti's inconstant eyes blinked exaggeratedly against the light, and then seemed all at once to have steadied into a new intensity. It was as if she were still recovering from the spell of darkness – widening her eyes, trying them out, bringing things back into focus. 'You'll be needing a drink after all that,' she said softly.

'No, Patti, that's fine. I'll be getting back.'

But she had grabbed a can of lager from the fridge, opened it, and was handing it to him. He could hardly wave it away now that it was open.

She was standing very close to him. 'Speaking of lips – '

'Were we?'

'I was reading about them. In one of my magazines. I read a lot, you know.'

'Nice to have the time.' Hallam swallowed as much cold lager as he could get down in one go.

She was between him and the way to the front door. 'Do you know anything about lips, John?'

'I know they cover your teeth.'

'Much more than that. For instance, did you know the lips are among the most sensitive parts of the human body? Thousands of little nerve endings connected to the brain. That's why we enjoy kissing so much.' Her voice was growing huskier; her breath was warm on his chin. 'In this article it was saying that people don't kiss enough. They should show their feelings more. A lot more. I think I'd agree with that – wouldn't you?'

She deftly took the can from his hand, pushed it on to a ledge behind her, and thrust her mouth softly but demandingly against his.

Hallam mumbled something, and found himself pinned to the wall.

'I have a very vivid imagination' – her lips parted and moved back an inch – 'and when I feel like it . . . dream about it . . .'

'Look, Patti –'

'Recently, I've been thinking a lot about . . . well, about you.'

Her lips were pressed against his again, more fiercely and more demandingly, when there was the scrape of Geoffrey's key in the lock.

When Kevin woke in the morning, everything felt strange. His bed was swaying soothingly a few inches from side to side. A gentle plashing sound threatened to send him to sleep again. He stretched luxuriously. He was in his new home: afloat in his houseboat.

He pushed the bedclothes back and swung his legs out, to find himself barefoot in a couple of inches of cold water. Gasping, he consoled himself with the thought that, with all this water supply available, at least the fire hazards ought not to be too awful.

Sally was just ahead of him when he reached Blackwall for the day shift. Every movement of her hips reminded him of that night, and the sizzling rhythm they had pounded out between them. He wanted to make the same music again, at the same tempo. It couldn't just be left as a one-off. She was too desirable for that.

He caught up with her. 'Had an inch of water all over the floor this morning. Maybe two.'

'It's called the deck, not the floor. Not going to sink, is it?'

'No, it's not. Look, I've got big plans for it. You'll have to come round once I've sorted it out, and – '

'Kev, can I stop you there? I hope you're not about to say "could do with a woman's touch". That would be very boring.'

'God, Sal, give us a break. I mean, I thought we might be getting something going. Bad enough getting my feet cold. No need for you to give me the cold shoulder as well.'

'Look, what happened that night was fun. I needed it. But that's it. Let's leave it.'

'But can't we just *talk*? Go to a pub or something? Like this evening, when we knock off. I mean, come on, what am I going to do? In public? Jump on you?'

'I'm not free tonight. Swimming practice. Got to try to redeem myself with the Brigade team.'

'Fair enough. So when?'

'I dunno. Tomorrow night?'

'Done. I could bring a bottle round. Or flowers.'

'I dunno,' she said again. 'Now I think of it, I'd meant to wash my hair.'

'Maybe I could help blow it dry.'

She studied him speculatively, sparing a wary glance at George Green and Recall as they ambled past.

'Oh, I dunno. Honestly, Kev, I'm not sure.'

Before she could get any closer to changing

her mind, he said: 'A bottle it is, then. Vodka O.K.?'

'Well . . . oh, well, not before eight o'clock, anyway.'

Billy was coming round from the yard after parking his hearse. Guiltily the two of them hurried in through the appliance bay.

Kevin decided to launch a two-pronged attack advance next evening: both vodka and flowers. He found them in the Pakistani shop which still struggled on against the competition of the supermarket, and on the dot of eight o'clock was climbing the stairs on the way to Sally's flat.

As he reached the head of the flight he could see light streaming from her open front door. It was an encouraging sign. She was ready and waiting for him, the door opened in welcome. Just as she would open in welcome before the night was out.

He had taken three steps along the balcony before becoming aware of a figure between him and the light, trying to bluster a way in.

'Eddie. I thought you were – '

'Oh, they turned me over, but I was clean.'

'Clean? Don't give me that crap. I've seen you using the stuff.'

'Not any more, Sal. Keeping fit and all that. Thought we might go swimming together.'

'Yeah? After your mates from the Drugs Squad popped round here? And you talk about being turned over. *And* you talk about swimming, which just happens to be a sore point at the moment, Eddie, because it happened the night before I was supposed to swim for the Brigade. They turn up, looking for you, or evidence, or whatever. And turn the place over: wreck it.'

'Sorry, Sal. I mean – '

'Eddie, I've heard it all before. I told you ages ago to get out of my life. So do just that.'

'Oh, come on, Sal, let me in. Let's talk about this.'

'No.'

Eddie began to lean on the door, forcing it further open inch by inch. More light flooded along the balcony.

Kevin swung forward. 'What's going on?'

Sally's eyes widened. 'Kevin, it's all right. Eddie's just going.'

'Who says I am?' Eddie's dark, scarred face turned to glare at Kevin. 'What's your game, mate? Why you sniffing round here with your bottle of booze? This is my girl.'

'I am not your girl.'

'No, she's not,' said Kevin. 'You heard her. She's had enough of you screwing up her life. So shift.'

'And who are you? The new man in her life?'

'No, he's not,' wailed Sally. 'Shut up, both of you.'

Eddie took a step towards Kevin. Kevin, not wanting to drop the vodka bottle, lowered his head and butted Eddie hard under the nose. He went down, spouting blood from his left nostril; and in a moment Sally was on her knees beside him, holding him down and raging at Kevin: 'You bloody idiot.'

Kevin stood over Eddie. 'Want some more?'

'Kevin, have you gone crazy?' Sally was cradling Eddie's head and dabbing with her handkerchief at his nose. 'Just get out of here – go on, out of here.'

'But Sal, I – '

'Kev, I don't want to know. Piss off!'

Kevin backed away. It was all too bloody unreasonable. And gradually he felt a slow rise of contempt, like a foul taste in his mouth. When he turned away and found himself passing a litter bin, he chucked the bottle of vodka in and was glad to hear it shatter.

Sandra was off to her class again, borne on a cloud of enthusiasm. Within a few evenings she had already acquired a mass of technological lingo which she eagerly repeated over breakfast, dinner, or whenever there was a free moment. John Hallam drew a sigh of relief when she had left the house and he could put his feet up at last.

Until the phone rang.

'Guess who?'

'Patti,' he protested, 'you shouldn't be ringing me.'

'It's all right. I know it's one of Sandra's evenings out.'

'Yes, but – '

'John, I keep thinking of what happened the other evening.'

'Patti, nothing happened the other evening. There's nothing to think about.'

'Why don't you nip round and see me? Right now.'

'Right now? And I suppose Geoffrey can contribute some useful tips?'

'Geoffrey's out at a Masonic meeting. Won't be back till late. John, I'm sure I can help you understand what's going on. I do know when men are attracted to me. It's chemistry. Nothing to be ashamed of. A secret between us.'

'Look, just cut this out, will you? And don't ring me at home. Or anywhere else.'

He slammed the receiver down and went back to his paper. It was difficult to concentrate. He tried the television instead, and when the phone began to ring again he turned the volume up to drown it out.

Sandra came in flushed with pride at having won her tutor's praise. She rattled off some more word processor terminology, and added: 'They've got very good contacts. There's a chance of me being recommended for a trial period with an advertising firm. At least that'll mean daytime work instead of evenings.'

The phone rang.

Hallam just managed to get there first. Patti's voice, ridiculously husky, said: 'She's not back yet, is she?'

'What? Oh, come off it.' Hallam assumed a bluff and breezy manner. 'Cut this out. And I've told you, stop ringing me at home. It's not on.'

Sandra was watching him, puzzled, as he put the receiver down. 'What was all that about?'

'Nothing. Er . . . just some geezer pestering me about charity football. Won't stop, some of them.'

'Didn't give him much time to get started, from what I heard.'

'Oh, I knew what he'd be on about. Heard it all before.'

No reason for her to look suspicious. No grounds for any suspicions whatsoever. Probably just his own imagination that she was looking at him oddly: damn it, he was feeling guilty when he had nothing to feel guilty about.

11

For two days Donald had been trying to summon up the courage to hold Billy to his promise. Each time he hoped to get him alone, there was that awful Mr Pearce in the way, glaring at him and telling him to push off. The rest of the lads didn't tell him to push off. They were nice. They gave him pictures of fire engines and old print-outs, and let him run errands for them. Especially Billy. But it was Billy who had made those promises. And this morning there was nobody about, and Billy oughtn't to keep him waiting any longer.

Donald crept across the forecourt and into the appliance bay with the newspaper.

'Good man.' Billy handed over the money. 'There you go.'

'Billy, don't you remember? You've kept saying you'd show me round the pump ladder. You promised.'

'What? Oh, well . . . we're a bit busy right now, see?'

'No you're not.'

Billy glanced over his shoulder at Kevin, on his way from the watchroom. 'Where's Poison?'

'Upstairs.'

Billy led Donald towards the cab of the pump ladder and helped him to climb in. It was super, sitting inside and leaning over the wheel, staring ahead and dreaming up a huge fire right over the rooftops.

'Can we have the two-tones on?'

'Better not,' said Billy nervously. 'Tell you what: you can have the blues on.' He indicated a switch on the dashboard.

'Right.' Donald still peered ahead. 'Where are we going?'

'Er . . . how about "Fire at Buckingham Palace, royal persons reported"? We gotta save them corgis!'

Donald went through the motions of driving the appliance forward and swinging out of the gates. Kevin, crossing the forecourt, mimed horror and leapt aside. They all laughed. It was great: oh, really great.

From inside they heard the bells go down; and the Blue Watch crew were sliding down the pole or dashing down the stairs. Sally, waving the print-out, sounded disbelieving: 'A *water* tower?'

Billy desperately dragged Donald from the cab

and was helping him down when Geoff Pearce erupted.

'Hey, you!'

Donald slid along the side of the appliance. 'I wasn't doing anything, Mr Pearce. Billy said I could.'

'Geoff, I was keeping my eye on him.'

Pearce loomed above Donald. 'I've told you before, young man. You're not allowed inside. It's dangerous. You hear me?'

'All right, Geoff, don't go on.'

Billy's plea was ignored. 'Get out of here. Out of the way. And don't come back.' And as Donald scurried away, ready to wait across the road to see the pump ladder race out, the awful threat followed him at the top of Mr Pearce's voice. 'Don't come back. Don't let me see you in here again. Never again – understood?'

Donald shrank back, watching the pump ladder as it swung into the street, but for once too wretched to thrill to the blues and two-tones. When it had wailed its way out of hearing, he couldn't bear to go home for tea. Mum and Louise would be able to tell he was upset, and he didn't want them fussing over him as if he were a little kid. He walked around until it was getting almost dark, and then headed for his own little private refuge.

The tower of the old Victorian pumping station thrust up from the coarse grass and rubble of an overgrown yard. It had been sealed off from the public by a corrugated iron fence; but not securely enough. The old double gates were firm enough, chained and padlocked together, but parts of the fence had sagged, and gaps between the corrugated sections had been forced wider by kids breaking through into the yard. Ground floor windows of the tall red-brick tower itself had been boarded up, and the imposing arch of the doorway filled in crudely with breeze blocks. There, too, time and vandals had taken their toll. One wooden panel had been wrenched from its sill with a crowbar, and there were dark holes into the interior.

One boy who had scrambled inside was now somewhere down the vast well in the centre of the tower.

The pump and pump ladder howled to a halt by the gates. Pearce jumped down with bolt cutters and freed the padlocked chain. It needed four of them to scrape the heavy gates open across the broken concrete so that the two appliances could get into the yard.

There was somebody there ahead of them: the boy's mother, who had raised the alarm, with two cowering boys who had obviously been involved in the escapade. Pearce tried to calm her by asking politely for her name, and for the boy's name, and saying as if it were a matter of everyday routine: 'It's all right, Mrs Knowles. We'll get Craig out, don't you worry.'

When John Hallam shone his torch down into the depths of the hole, the rest of them felt a lot less confident. There had been a metal cover, but the boys had dragged this aside to reveal an iron girder across the top, and a rusted metal ladder going sheer down one side.

Nick Georgiadis said: 'Right. Bring in the generator and floodlights. We're going to need more light down there. And John, contact Control and get someone over from the water company. And find out as fast as possible what sort of depth we're dealing with.' Mrs Knowles and the two boys had crept in behind the firefighters, shrinking back against the wall. He turned to them. 'Now, lads. You definitely saw Craig go in, did you?'

They gulped and nodded.

'He couldn't just have gone off somewhere, and you only *thought* he'd fallen?'

They shook their heads.

'You'd better be telling the truth, Pete,' cried Mrs Knowles. 'Or I'll bloody well kill you.'

Nick held up a warning hand. 'Did you hear a splash or anything?'

Close to tears, the boys shook their heads again.

Sicknote and George carried the generator in, followed by Billy and Kevin with flood lamps.

Hard on their heels came John Hallam. 'Control have been in touch with the water company, guv. They reckon it's a single shaft, two hundred feet deep, with sixty feet of water. No side tunnels, no ledges. And there's no way down except from the top.'

'Are they sending someone?'

'On his way. But the thing is, guv, they said they never send men down these wells. There's an oxygen deficiency.'

'And that kid's down there?' The station officer watched grimly as Billy began lowering one of the lights on the end of a long line, picking out the sour green moss on the brickwork.

'There!' Billy braced himself by gripping the girder, and leaned out over the well-head. 'Look, guv – you can just make something out.'

There was a dim white shape in the darkness. It must have been a good hundred feet or so down.

Hallam and Georgiadis crouched at the edge, talking in an undertone as Pearce prevented the distraught Mrs Knowles from rushing forward.

'It's a hell of a long way down,' muttered Hallam.

'Sixty feet of water at the bottom. Even if by some chance he's survived the fall and is managing to stay afloat, we've been told there's very little oxygen. Probably something else very unpleasant.'

Kevin came carefully up behind them. 'The Fire Rescue Unit's here, guv. Think we can send some-one down?'

'Without oxygen? You couldn't fit a man and B.A. down there. No space. Impossible.'

'We could if we joined five or six decom lines together and kept the air cylinder at the top.'

It was a dangerous proposition: separating the mask from the cylinders and sending a man down on a line offered so many chances of a failure – the line getting snagged, or punctured, the mask tearing away . . .

And what would they use for a pulley?

'Let's see what the F.R.U. think about it.'

Within two minutes a breeze block had been smashed out of the archway and a line led through the opening from the back of the pump. At a signal from Hallam, Recall accelerated forward and the wall collapsed in a cloud of dust. He pulled out of the way while the scattered blocks were manhandled to one side. Bayleaf reversed the pump ladder slowly through the gaping archway and manoeuvred it to the edge of the well.

George and Sally began unloading B.A. sets. Billy laid out a salvage sheet by the side of the wall, and more lighting was positioned to tilt beams down into the shaft. Pearce set to work separating the face mask of a B.A. from the cylinder, and one of the F.R.U. men came to help with reconnecting it to a series of joined-up airlines. Sicknote and Recall made lowering lines ready from the appliance ladder. Kevin, wondering why he had been so mad as to suggest this operation, started to fit himself into a sling formed from a loop on the end of the line, tied off with a parachute knot. He reached for the B.A. mask.

Then Georgiadis said: 'Sorry, Kevin, this one's down to me.'

'Oh no, guv. It was my idea, and – '

'Out of there quick. No argument.'

Now that it had come to it, Kevin very much wanted to argue. He was scared stiff; but it had certainly been his idea and he wanted to see it through. But under the station officer's basilisk stare, he grudgingly freed himself from the sling and handed over the mask.

Georgiadis was emptying his pockets. He handed the contents, his Evac and, after a brief hesitation, his white helmet to Hallam. 'If I don't need it any more, you can flog it.'

'One previous owner.' Hallam forced a grin. 'Good working order.'

Georgiadis fitted himself into the sling and put the mask on. Pearce turned the valve on the air cylinder. The station officer gave a thumbs-up sign, and Kevin and George carefully inverted him over the well, hanging down head first, while Sicknote and Recall organized the lowering lines. Kevin handed one over for attaching to the boy down below . . . if that pale shape was really something that could be salvaged.

'Right. Ready. Start lowering.'

Recall and Sicknote began slowly paying out the lines. The whole crew peered over the edge as Georgiadis disappeared down the well. Hallam called four of them back to get the extension ladders off the pump and laid across the sides of the hole.

In the patchwork of light and shadow playing across the walls of the shaft, Nick Georgiadis suddenly tugged on the signal line to stop them lowering him into a cluster of loose pipework. They could just see his hand pushing the pipes back very gingerly, to avoid dislodging anything which might fall down on Craig. After a pause he tugged twice on the line, and continued his painfully slow descent. Inch by inch he went; then several feet, and more and more, without giving any further signals.

Hallam's voice was hoarse. 'How much line do we have left?'

Kevin glanced apprehensively at the ladder above. 'Fifteen feet, sub. He must be getting on for a hundred feet down by now.'

Silence fell over Blue Watch and the paramedic who had come in from his ambulance.

There was a double tug on the line.

Everybody tensed; and waited.

They could only guess at what might be going on down there. It was unlikely that Craig could have fallen into the foul water and still be swimming around. But if he had hit more pipework or a girder, he might have been killed immediately.

There were two tugs on the line. Then a third. As

they began hauling up, there was weight on both lines. But Pearce was leaning across the cylinder to say, without Mrs Knowles hearing: 'Only five more minutes' supply left, sub.'

Hallam jerked a thumb at Kevin and his assistants on the lines. 'Quick as you can.'

They speeded up. Bayleaf and George climbed on to the ladders across the well, squatting ready to help as soon as Craig was lifted close enough.

'Here they come!'

Mrs Knowles sobbed as Sally put an arm round her and steadied her. Craig, suspended on the second line, was slowly manoeuvred between the girder and ladders. George got his arms round the limp form, eased it on to the ladder, and backed cautiously away to the solid rim of the well. Two paramedics were waiting with a resuscitator and a stretcher.

The rest of Blue Watch turned back to heave their station officer out on to the surround of the well. Hallam pulled the mask off. Georgiadis looked utterly exhausted, but tried to lift his head and look enquiringly at the men carrying the stretcher away.

'He's still breathing, guv,' Hallam reassured him.

Georgiadis was still limp by the time they got back to the station, but when Hallam was helping him out of the pump ladder cab he summoned up the energy to say: 'Kevin.'

'Guv?'

'That was quick thinking back there.'

'Just takes brains, guv. Some of us have 'em, some don't.'

'All right, all right, so you do have 'em. Just as well for young Craig.'

Coming from the station officer, that was as much of a compliment as anyone could ever expect. Kevin walked round the side of the pump ladder, busying himself with checking that everything was secure just in case anyone saw him looking too pleased with himself.

He came face to face with George Green, and on impulse blurted out: 'Come and have a drink in the boat tomorrow evening, George? Sort of christen it . . . her?'

'Sorry, mate, I can't make it.'

'Oh, come on. Billy's bringing this new find of his, Lauren – you know, the one he picked up when the guv'nor sent them on that restaurant F.P. check, and found it had turned into a strip club.'

'You'll be all right for cabaret, then.'

'So you'll come?'

'I'd like to, but honest, I've got a . . . well, prior business engagement, sort of.'

Recall leaned round the end of the pump. 'I don't happen to have a prior engagement.'

'Nor me,' said Bayleaf.

'Oh, well, the more the merrier.' As they made

their way into the station, Kevin caught up with Sally. 'My houseboat-warming party – you coming? Tomorrow evening?'

'No,' said Sally. 'Sorry. No can do.'

'But why not come along? I'm rounding up most of the rest of 'em.'

'Kevin, please. I've got swimming, O.K.? End of subject.'

'Look, Sal, what's wrong? I mean, if it's the other night, and your precious Eddie – '

'You nearly broke his nose.'

'I thought I was doing you a good turn.'

'Well, you weren't. So now will you leave me alone?'

Sicknote drifted towards them. 'What's this about breaking champagne over the bows of some luxury liner?'

Geoff Pearce was making a slow circuit of the appliance, his head cocked. If there was one thing Kevin would least sooner have aboard than an albatross it was Geoff Pearce.

'See you later,' he hissed to Sicknote.

Sally walked briskly away.

Billy, as promised, brought the bosomy blonde he had acquired at the strip club when the team had supposedly been concentrating on a fire precautions inspection. Lauren could herself have lit many a fire in many a manly breast. In spite of his wife's presence, Sicknote introduced himself as

Bert Quigley and, presumably in a charitable desire to make her feel at home, turned on all his social graces.

Kevin was passing out cans of lager. 'There you go, Sicknote.'

Lauren stared. 'Why do they call you Sicknote? I thought you just said your name was Bert.'

'Well, firefighters are famous for nicknames, you see.'

'Yeah, but why Sicknote?'

'I really can't remember. Lost in the mists of time, you could say.'

She eyed him shrewdly. 'You always sick or something?'

'No. no. I'm very healthy, actually.'

'Why is it, then? Is it your hair?'

Sicknote flinched. 'My hair?'

'Yeah. Is it to do with losing your hair?'

'Oh, I don't . . . I . . . er . . .'

'Surprised they don't call you Kojak!'

Lauren was shrieking with laughter as Bayleaf and Clare appeared at the head of the companionway. Kevin renewed his attacks on the tops of lager cans. Each newcomer diminished the available space in the cabin. Elbows jostled, cans of lager sloshed about and splashed on to the table and the floor.

Clare and Jean moved closer together and began inspecting the compact kitchen units with a mixture of doubt and approval.

'She's beginning to get interested,' said Bayleaf. 'I was afraid it wasn't going to click.'

'Interested?' Kevin took a few minutes off to lean against the bulkhead.

'We're going to be a bit involved in kitchens ourselves pretty soon.'

'Moving?'

'Eventually. We've just bought a restaurant.'

John Hallam joined them. 'You've done what?'

'Like I said, bought a restaurant. Living accommodation over it. Partners with another bloke.'

'Bit sudden, isn't it?'

'Well, he came to us with a good offer and we went for it. Clare's money, really. She was left it by her first husband's mother. I mean, it's nothing posh. Just a sort of seaside place. You know, prawn cocktail, steak and chips.'

'That's better than you ever dish out in the mess.' Sicknote had added himself to the group.

Kevin reached for a plate on the shelf above, and shoved a a ham roll at him.

John Hallam said: 'Just a minute. You aiming to leave the Brigade?'

'When I'm good and ready,' said Bayleaf.

They were all looking at him with some disquiet. Kevin was half tempted to ask if there were any vacancies on the staff: a job of that kind would make a welcome change from the inexorable routine of two days on, two nights on, four days off, two days on . . .

'Where is this place?' asked Recall.

'Littlehampton.'

'That's where Billy comes from, isn't it?'

Lauren's cackling laugh erupted again. Before Billy could come up with an answer, there was another call from the doorway above: a cooing yet discordant call. 'Better late then never, eh?'

Kevin froze, speechless. How the hell had Geoff and Patti Pearce cottoned on to the timing of the party – and why the hell did they suppose they'd be welcome?

A few minutes later Sandra said: 'Must get away early, Kev. I've got an interview first thing tomorrow. Don't want to reel in with bloodshot eyes and fluff the whole thing.'

There was an awkward silence after Hallam and Sandra had gone. Over the next thirty minutes people gradually drifted away: all except Billy and Lauren, who did not so much drift as dash, after Billy had pinched her bottom and muttered something in her ear. Kevin assumed the comfortably equipped hearse had been parked not so very far away from the waterside.

Geoff and Patti were the last to leave. Bidding them a thankful goodnight, Kevin went round the cabin clearing the empties into a bin bag, and mopping surfaces to clear them of lager and crumbs.

He had almost finished when there were footsteps on the tow-path outside, stopping right beside his boat. He waited for someone to appear in the doorway – Sicknote, saying he had left his cap behind, or something of that sort.

There was no further sound. Kevin climbed out on deck; and was at once seized and dragged on to the tow-path.

Two dark faces moved closer to his. 'Kevin Medhurst?'

'What's this about?'

He was punched hard in the stomach. As he tried to struggle free and lash out himself, his arms were pinioned behind his back, and another couple of punches thudded into his stomach. Then he was lifted bodily and hurled into the canal. A voice jeered after him: 'Eddie sends his regards.'

12

The stage doorman was a small, wiry man in his sixties. He was a keen talker, buttonholing performers as they arrived for each show – even when, as at present, most of them were Russian and could not understand a word he said – and eagerly swapping reminiscences with George Green because of their similar background. Tommy had been in the Brigade himself until invalided out in 1968, and was sure the whole outfit had gone to rack and ruin since then. Although, out of politeness and the urge to chat, he was prepared to be matey to George, he still insisted each evening on summing up the rules and regulations just to make sure their temporary fireman was reliable. *Reliable*: George heard the echo of his father's grumblings.

The job in fact was a lot less troublesome than any which Kelly's relations had thrown his way. At the beginning of the evening he had to inspect the fire alarms, fire buckets and emergency phone, and unlock a sequence of foyer, auditorium and fire doors. Contents of the first-aid box had to be checked each time in spite of not having been used during the last three productions. If there was a fire, George was supposed to put it out promptly with the aid of the sprinkler system, CO^2 and BCF extinguishers at the front and back of the house, and buckets of sand in the foyer and the backs of the dress circle and gallery. If it got out of hand, he must call the Fire Brigade. He prayed that this wouldn't happen: he wanted no further stories circulating around Blackwall and Shadbrook.

This evening he had completed the routine before the first dancers arrived. He contrived to be near the stage door, pretending to listen to Tommy chuntering on, as they came in. At the same time he was pretending to himself that it was purely a matter of routine that he should have positioned himself here, just as later he would stand unobtrusively at the side of the foyer as the audience came in.

She was late. The performers were all supposed to be delivered to the stage door simultaneously by a coach from their hotel; but either the prima ballerina was a law unto herself, or she had been practising her English on the coach driver. When she did at last come in through the stage door, there were little touches of rose on the pale, almost translucent skin drawn over her high cheekbones.

She caught George's gaze on her, offered him a shy hint of a smile, and hurried past. Even walking in flat, practical shoes her movements were as graceful as when she was dancing on stage.

Crazy, hanging about like this: like a moonstruck teenager. She could never be more than a distant, hazy dream. Her name was Larissa, that much he knew from her picture in the glass frame at the entrance and from the theatre programme, but it could not be the name of a real flesh and blood woman – only the name of a fleeting dream, way beyond his reach.

Yet when he stood in the wings at the beginning of the performance, pretending again – this time that it was essential he should be keeping an eye on the lighting panel and the switches for the sprinklers – she was briefly real, the flesh of her arms and neck glowing as they rose from the skimpy ballet costume. She shifted her weight gently on to her right foot, and folded and unfolded her arms like the wings of a swan, almost brushing George's shoulder.

'Good luck,' he said.

She smiled again, and floated out on to the stage.

He had never imagined himself wasting even five minutes of his time watching ballet. It was still odd to see a man in tights like that skimming about the stage and making slithery movements with his arms; but when the hero and heroine came together and the girl was lifted ecstatically into the air and held there, he knew in his own bones what strength that needed, even though she looked so slim and ethereal, moving so lightly that she might have been quite weightless.

When the applause rolled up out of the stalls and seemed to puff the dancer offstage into the wings past him, he persuaded himself that her remote, practised smile was meant for him.

'Quite a bird,' said Tommy behind him. Oh, like a bird all right – but not in that way, not in Tommy's tone of voice. 'We've had some crackers here in my time. Wish I was your age again, I can tell you.'

George went off on patrol.

He had taken only a few steps along the corridor to the dressing-rooms when there was a scream. Smoke was pouring out of Larissa's dressing-room as she opened the door. She cried out something in what he supposed was Russian, and plunged into the room.

'Hold it!' He flung himself forward.

A towel had been draped over the back of a chair to dry in front of the bars of an electric heater. It was smouldering, emitting a choking grey cloud. As George reached the door, the girl was reaching for a vase, pulling out flowers and poised to hurl the water over the towel and the heater.

'No!'

George lunged forward, grabbed the vase from her hand, and stooped to switch off the heater. Then he ran water into the basin in the corner of the room, picked up the towel, and dropped it in. There was an angry hiss and a last gout of stinking smoke. He opened the window and turned back towards her. 'Never pour water over an electrical fire.'

'I know.' She struggled for words in English. 'It is . . . foolish . . . stupid of me. I get scared. I am stupid, yes.'

'Well' – he moved the heater further from the cramped dressing-table and with a meaningful look emptied the vase – 'it's all right now. You can relax.'

'I must thank you.' Her long, bare arms made a slow arching movement like the neck of that swan she must have danced so often. 'What . . . please, your name?'

He couldn't understand why he had so much difficulty in pronouncing it. 'George.'

'George.' She made it sound so much more musical. 'I am Larissa.'

'I know.'

'Thank you, George.' She kissed him on the cheek. 'I think you save my life.'

That night he hung about waiting to see her off the premises, this time basking in her unrestrained, ravishing smile, and then automatically went through the sequence of checking the auditorium, bars and corridors, and locking up.

When he got home he was still wrapped in fantasy, and wanted only to slide into bed and lie awake for a brief dream, or drop down into a longer, more vivid dream.

Kelly was awake, waiting for him. As he undressed she asked: 'What are you thinking about?'

'Nothing much.' He was scared that if he turned towards her the imprint of Larissa's grateful kiss would somehow still be glowing there.

'How was the theatre?'

'All right. Funnily enough, had a fire. In the ballerina's dressing-room.'

'And what were you doing in the ballerina's dressing-room?'

'Putting the fire out, of course.'

She humped herself into a position which looked more uncomfortable than the first. Enviously she asked: 'What are they like, then, the dancers?'

'Oh, I don't know. I'm only a fireman. They don't talk to me.'

She wasn't going to be so easily satisfied. 'We used to like dancing, didn't we?' she wheedled.

'Amateur ballroom. That's slightly different, love.'

'George, how long are you going to go on working nights?'

Her voice was beginning to rasp on his nerves; so different from that lilting, foreign accent. He could have gone on listening to Larissa all night. 'I've hardly even started. And you know how long. Until I've paid back your blasted brother, and moved us to a decent flat.'

'But it's five nights a week. And when you're not round there, you've got your nights on duty. I'm getting fed up with being left alone here all the time.'

'What am I supposed to do? You think I enjoy going to a poxy theatre all night?'

'Yes,' said Kelly searchingly, 'I do.'

Nick had been invited to Kevin's party, but had begged off. It was not that he felt, as some station officers and folk like Scase did, that one should not mix too freely with the men. He was happy to join in some functions, charity bashes, and special celebrations. But tonight he was not in the mood. Always at the back of his mind nowadays was the haunting, taunting image of Ariadne. He thought of Petros pawing her; and then forced himself not to think of it. On the day of her marriage he had told himself that this was final, it was all over, there was nothing to think about any more. And after that final tempestuous confrontation in the church so few days before her wedding, Ariadne must surely have felt the same.

Only he knew this was not true. What was the use of repeating it over and over again when it was all cancelled out by those long-distance calls? A woman on honeymoon had been sneaking every opportunity of phoning another man – phoning him here at home, even getting in touch with him on duty – sometimes chattering breathlessly about nothing in particular and then stopping in mid-sentence as if his voice were the only thing in the world she wanted to hear. And sometimes saying that things were even more depressing than she had expected, and they must meet and talk the moment she got back.

They must certainly not meet and talk. Every encounter in the past had meant trouble and self-questioning; or worse dangers. He still had to exercise some self-control, even if Ariadne couldn't.

He wondered if she would phone again this evening.

Maybe it would have been better if he had gone to Kevin's party after all. Sitting here alone, he would be spending the hours telling himself he hoped she wouldn't be silly enough to call; and at the same time he would be impatient for her to call.

There were only two inches left in the bottle of ouzo. He wondered whether to go round to Uncle Dimitri's and have a meal and a bottle of wine. But Uncle Dimitri would be sure to comment on him sitting alone. That was something else he wanted to stop.

And he might miss Ariadne's call.

The doorbell buzzed into the silence.

It was an odd time for anyone to be rolling up. Nick opened the door with no idea who he might expect to find there.

Ariadne stood framed in the opening: tanned,

very warm and beautiful, her usually tightly coiled black hair loose over her shoulders. She waved a duty-free bag at him, with a wine bottle sticking out of the top.

'Brought you a present.'

'I thought you weren't coming back until next week.'

'We had to come back early. Petros's mother is not too well. She wants to go back home to Cyprus, but she doesn't want to go alone, so he is being her good little boy and patting her hand right this moment.' She swung the bag with its wine bottle gently towards him. 'Can I bring this in?'

'Do you think you should?'

'No. But are you going to lock me out?'

He stood aside to let her pass. Just the slightest movement of her shoulder was fatal – fatal for both of them.

She tossed the bag towards the couch, not caring whether the bottle broke or not. Her hand clawed desperately at him, and the quiver of her haunches sent a wild pulse through him.

'We shouldn't be doing this,' he protested absurdly. 'It's crazy.'

'I know.'

They both knew it and meant it; but it did not stop them for more than a few more seconds.

Before morning roll-call the members of Blue Watch wandered in and out of the locker room, thanking Kevin for the party. One or two glanced curiously at his bleary eyes and the scratch on his cheek where he had hauled himself out of the water on to the canal bank, but his expression did not encourage them to ask questions. It was left to George to come out with it. 'Blimey, that must have been one hell of a party.'

'Yeah, I could've done with you there.'

They assembled for roll-call. The moment they had fallen out for their duties and Sally was heading for the door of the pump ladder, Kevin crossed the bay and caught up with her. 'I want a word with you.'

'What about?'

'About your friends. Lovely crowd, aren't they? Eddie's twin brother and some illegal immigrant who does whatever he's told?'

'What are you on about?'

He told her, and finished: 'As if you didn't know.'

'Oh, look now. So Eddie's mates chuck you in the canal and you think it's down to me? Great.'

'I notice you weren't keen on coming to my party. Maybe you were ordered to leave the coast clear.'

'I didn't come to your party because I was going swimming. I told you that.'

'You wouldn't have come anyway. Because for some reason these days you're treating me like something the dog dragged in.'

'Because I don't care to be regarded as a bitch

permanently on heat, just for your pleasure. And also, Kevin, I don't like violence. Hate it.'

'You can talk, after last night.'

'Last night was nothing to do with me and you know it. Look, Kevin. Like I said, I don't approve of violence. Not what happened last night and not what you did to Eddie the other night either. I hate it all. But you bloody started it, don't forget that.'

'That's really nice, that is. I was trying to help you.'

'So you keep saying. But if you want to help me, Kevin, just leave me alone.'

Geoff Pearce trotted in his usual fussy way out of the watchroom. 'Just wanted to say how Patti and I enjoyed ourselves last night, Kevin.'

Glad somebody did: Kevin nearly said it out loud. Though the Pearces were in fact the last people about whose enjoyment he could give a damn one way or the other.

13

'Guess who?'

John Hallam instinctively edged further along the passage, away from the open kitchen door.

'You never stop trying, do you?' he improvised.

'John, this is one of Sandra's evenings out, isn't it?'

'No, it's not.' From the corner of his eye he was aware of Sandra in the kitchen doorway. 'No,' he said loudly. 'We'll sort it. Not right now. And not when I'm on duty, either. All right? Yeah, and you. See you.'

Sandra said: 'And who was that?'

'Jimmy. Got more front than Brighton, that bloke.'

'He's not the only one, then, is he?'

'Mm?' said Hallam innocently.

'I said he's not the only one. If it was him at all.'

'Who else would it be?'

'Oh, I don't know. How about Patti Pearce? She's been on the phone a bit lately, hasn't she? I think you've got some explaining to do.'

'Sandra, what on earth – '

'And darling Patti's got a lot to explain, as well. Let's have it all at one go, shall we?'

'I don't know what you're on about.'

'Mysterious phone calls.' Sandra was catapulting the words at him. 'Heavy breathing. Then we get cut off.'

'Heavy breathing? You mean you've had one of *those* ringing you? Why didn't you tell me?'

'Come off it, John. Each time that phone rings lately you've been making a sprint for it. And when I'm the one who answers, I could swear I recognize who's doing the breathing. What's been going on when my back's been turned?'

'Nothing.'

'Very romantic nothings, maybe?'

'Me? And Patti? Oh, all right, she may have got some weird ideas in her head. But not me.' He couldn't believe Sandra was struggling into her coat and preparing for battle. 'Look, I'm telling you, if there's anything at all, it's all in her head.'

'So let's get it out of her head right now.'

'You're not going round there – at this time of night?'

'I am.'

'What's that going to look like?'

'If you really want to know, you can come and find out.'

All he could do was grab his jacket and follow her, though he had no idea how he was going to stop a confrontation or even limit the damage.

Geoff Pearce answered the door, looking briefly pleased. It was the first time they had troubled to come round here. The beginnings of his smile evaporated at Sandra's strident tone of voice. 'Is Patti in?'

'Of course. Come in.' As he closed the door behind them, he said with forced joviality: 'Bit late for socializing, isn't it?'

'I'm sorry, Geoff,' Hallam attempted. 'We really shouldn't be here like this.'

'Like what?'

Sandra said: 'I want a word with your wife, Geoffrey.'

Patti slid out round the sitting-room door, her eyes wandering, more as if she were listening alertly than looking for anything in particular. 'I'm right here, Sandra. What's wrong?'

Hallam stuck out a protesting hand towards his wife. He could have saved himself the trouble. Nothing would have stopped her now. 'I'll tell you what's wrong. *You* are. Trying to seduce my husband right under my nose. Very wrong, Patti – d'you understand that?'

Geoff Pearce gave his wife a quick, dismal glance.

She looked far from dismal. The accusation seemed to have brought a flush of appreciation rather than indignation to her cheeks.

'Look.' Hallam made a last despairing attempt to nip the whole row in the bud. 'This whole thing is out of order. Let's sleep on it, shall we?'

'Yes,' purred Patti, 'you'd like to, wouldn't you? I found that out quick enough.'

Sandra was taken aback. This was not quite the response she had expected. Before she could say anything, Pearce was intervening. He had the air of supporting the intruders rather than his wife. 'Patti, I think John's right. This isn't the time or place for this kind of thing.'

'That's what I said at the time, for all the good it did.'

Sandra got her breath back. 'What's she talking about?'

'It's all a misunderstanding,' said Hallam. 'There never was anything in it.'

Pearce sounded just as helpless. 'Leave it there, Patti, will you? Let's all just leave it there.'

'What's the matter with you?' Sandra demanded. 'Your wife gets the hots for my husband and you don't care?'

'If John says there's nothing in it,' said Pearce, 'I'm prepared to believe him. There isn't, is there, John?'

'Of course there isn't. This whole thing's blown up out of nothing.' Hallam turned more confidently to Sandra. 'No point in fighting over something that didn't happen.'

She looked far from convinced. But she was ready to go, after delivering a parting shot. 'I don't know what's going on with you two, but I've said what I came to say. Just keep your hands off my husband in future, all right?'

'I think you've got the wrong end of the stick, Sandra,' said Patti silkily. 'Strange, you and your husband. I've often wondered about the two of you. I wonder how you got this way?'

On the doorstep Sandra took Hallam's arm, though without much affection. 'At least I believe you this time. Must be quite hard to fancy a woman like that.' She virtually dragged him along the short path to the gate.

In the morning there was no sign of Pearce waiting for a lift. As they stood down in the evening, Hallam automatically slowed to pick him up on the way out. 'Look, Geoff, about last night – '

'Probably best if we just forget about it, John. It wasn't your fault.'

'No, well, but – '

'I'd rather just leave it, if you don't mind.'

Pearce walked off towards the bus stop.

Diana had phoned him at the station and was waiting at a corner table in the tea-shop, strategically placed between the better end of Blackwall and a long avenue out into leafier suburbs. It had so far resisted calling itself Ye Olde Tea-Shoppe, but might not hold out much longer.

Without preamble Diana said: 'Just what's going on? I think some explanations are called for.'

'I don't think I owe anybody any explanations.'

'Only half the Greek population of London.' She paused to order tea and cakes, then went on: 'All right, I'll spell it out for you. Because I'm worried. Ariadne's not happy. And she can't hide it. When I saw her looking at you at the wedding – and the way I've seen her since – I know it's not over. I know a lot more than that, Nick.'

'What's this, woman's intuition?'

'I see her at that school, remember. We use the same premises for art classes. And I've seen her in tears more often than not. And she clams up whenever I mention your name. Something's going on, isn't it?'

'What difference does it make to you?'

'She's my friend.'

'That's it, is it? That's the only reason you're interested in my part in it?'

Her lips parted, and he remembered how they had parted at the approach of his mouth; and thought how odd it was that it should be so meaningless now.

'All right,' said Diana, 'it rankles.'

'I don't see why it should. You were the one who wouldn't make the commitment.'

'Hold on, Nick. I was barely out of one situation

and you were pushing me into another. Just to blot out what you really longed for?'

'It's all in the past, anyway,' he said.

'What is – me or Ariadne?'

They sat silent as the waitress fussed with cups, saucers, plates and a silver-plated cake dish. When the girl had gone, Nick said: 'I don't know how it's got like this. Honest. I really don't. I thought I was over her. I thought she was over me. I know it's completely out of order, too, but that doesn't stop it. It's real. Much more real than I ever wanted it to be.'

'Doesn't exactly fit with career man either, does it? You've got a family like the Mafia, and *she's* a married woman.'

He nodded. 'Perfect, isn't it?'

Diana toyed with a chocolate éclair. Wiping the cream and chocolate from her lips occupied her for a few moments, but did not distract her from her accusations. 'So what are you going to do about it?'

'I wish to God I knew. But I see her and I want her, and I don't want to let her go – '

'But you did. You had your chance, and you let her go.'

'You sound like the family. All right, I get the message. It's just a mess, and it's been my own doing. Still, at least I've said it to somebody. I'm glad you rang. Thanks.'

Her sympathy was fading fast. 'Well, I was always the consolation prize, wasn't I? Something to take the two of you off each other's minds. Then I just happened to get awkward and show I have one of my own. What a shame for you both.'

'Don't think like that. She didn't plan it like that, nor did I. Don't think that.'

'Why not, if it's true?' Diana bent down to retrieve her handbag, and began to get up ready to leave. 'I must admit I was curious, apart from being hurt. Now at least I know.'

'Diana, don't go.'

'Don't worry, Nick. I'm not going to run off and tell everybody. But don't start looking for more consolation, because there isn't any. You have to sort this out for yourself.'

'Sure. Just tell me how.'

'That's your problem. I'll see you.' She had gone a few steps before she looked back and said: 'On second thoughts, I won't. 'Bye, Nick.'

He wanted to follow her and explain something. But since he couldn't explain it honestly to himself, what chance did he stand of putting it across to Diana?

It would be a relief to be back on duty, where most of the problems he had to face were purely technical, not emotional ones. That was what he was cut out for. He kept telling himself that; and the image of Ariadne kept swimming up to mock such pretensions.

It was only a hundred yards from home, and sometimes his sister was allowed in to bring him a flask of coffee and some chocolate biscuits; but it was still his own very special place, and Mum and Louise understood this and were quite happy so long as they knew where he was, and Louise could check that the warehouse and its staircase were still safe. The building was derelict, but good and solid. Donald had taken over what must have been a storeman's cubby-hole on the top floor, complete with a large table in the middle of the room. The whole place looked even smaller than it really was, crammed with the bits and pieces he had collected over the years: outmoded firemen's uniforms, fire safety posters, two Lego fire engines, a noticeboard with strips of telex paper scrounged from Blue Watch shouts, and some old training manuals. He had never been able to memorize anything at all at school, yet he knew the manuals off by heart, word for word.

Pride of place went to the model on the table: from shoe boxes and cardboard he had constructed a replica of Blackwall Fire Station and part of the street, coloured in with felt pens, and kept adding to it. There were some toy railway porters he had re-coloured to turn them into firefighters, and although their faces were hard to tell apart he knew which one was Billy, and which one Kevin, and Bayleaf and all the rest of them. He had even introduced Mr Pearce, but at this moment he didn't care to look at him. Mr Pearce was horrid, all set to spoil everything.

Trying to get back in the right mood, he spent a

few minutes pushing the two appliances in and out, and shoved some of the blue figures around to do maintenance. It still wasn't coming to life the way it usually did. It had never let him down before. He began to get frightened.

Staring at the station, he whispered: 'Please come out.' His imagination often coaxed the engines into motion, and he could sit back and visualize them racing down the street, round the corner, on their way towards something down by the river or in a smoky back street. But this evening they refused to come alive.

They would have to learn there was a real fire. And right on their own doorstep. That would wake them up.

Donald reached for the bottle of methylated spirits under the table, and poured some into one of the cardboard houses. When it was well and truly soaked, he struck a match and tossed it in. Pink and purple flames licked up from the interior. He was turning a short length of hose towards them when there came the faint but unmistakable sound of two-tones not far away. He dropped the hose and went to open the window, hoping to see the wonderful red monsters in the street below. A strong breeze carried the sound into the room for a few seconds; but then the siren faded into the distance.

When Donald turned back into the room, he found what else the breeze had done. His whole model was ablaze from end to end.

As he grabbed the hose, one whole section of the model was blown on to the plywood and card he had stacked on the floor ready for the next building extension. He tried to get at it and kick it aside, but succeeded only in dislodging the bottle of meths. It shattered, and suddenly there was a lake of fire spreading across the floor.

He edged round the blaze with his back to the wall, and reached the door.

As he opened it, the wind intensified. Smoke swirled round his head, blinding him. He groped for the stair rail, but couldn't find it, and felt himself staggering back towards the room. Liquid fire streamed past him and dripped over the edge of the landing to the floor below. Dry, dusty debris seemed to blaze up of its own accord to meet the falling driblets of flame.

It would be all right. Blue Watch wouldn't let him down.

He heard the sound of them coming. They would unwind the hoses and come in through the ground floor and haul the hoses up the stairs, killing the fire as they came.

But he couldn't stand here any longer, waiting for them. There was too much smoke. He had to get out in the open or he'd be choked. As he groped his way out on to the external staircase, there was a shout.

It was his friend Recall. 'Look – there's someone up there.'

He was going to wave and call back, but then there

came another voice: an awful voice. 'It's that bloody kid Donald. What's he doing?' Mr Pearce, shouting as usual. And starting to come up the metal stairs.

Donald began to back unsteadily away, then turned and went upwards step by step.

'Donald,' Recall was yelling, 'stay right there. We'll be with you in a sec.'

He would have stopped and waited; but it was Pearce who was coming up first, and he wasn't going to stop and wait for that horrible man to get at him. He reached the top of the flight and stepped on to the flat roof, edging round a skylight frame and into the shelter of a water tank.

'Donald' – it was Pearce again – 'where are you?'

Donald wanted to stay quite still, but at the same time he wanted to run: only there was nowhere to run to. He peered round the corner of the tank, made a brief dash towards a ventilation housing, and came face to face with Pearce.

'Donald. It's all right. Come here.'

Donald backed away.

'Donald, come here! Over here. Keep away from the edge!'

Donald took one further step backwards, and felt something sag and give way beneath his feet. Now there was nothing to tread on, nothing to hold him up. He was falling, the buildings and sky and gouts of flame were going round and over and under . . . until he hit the ground, and then there was nothing at all any more.

14

John Hallam had had just about enough. There had been times when he grumbled about having been conned into giving Geoff Pearce lifts in and out of the station on a regular basis. Now he was furious that three times in a row Pearce had brushed aside his offer and, finishing a shift, ostentatiously headed for the bus stop. Half the Watch must have noticed by now, and would be muttering questions about what exactly was in the wind.

For a few days you might have attributed it to Pearce being upset over what had happened to poor Donald, and not wanting to talk about it in the intimacy of the car. There'd be questions to answer at the coroner's inquest; and there ought to be a lot of awkward questions flitting about in Pearce's own guilty mind – questions about his own attitude to the lad, and what that might have contributed to the death fall. But there was more to it than that.

Before it got out of hand, Hallam determined to get the matter settled. Coming off at nine o'clock on the Wednesday morning, he drew in at the bus stop where Pearce was standing second in a small queue, and leaned over to open the passenger door. 'Come on, Geoff. Hop in.'

'I'm fine, thanks, John.'

'No, you're not.' When Pearce still made no move but pretended to be squinting down the street in the hope of seeing a bus, Hallam leaned over as far as he could and spoke in a clear, calculated undertone. 'Either you get in and we have this out right now, or tomorrow I go and ask the guv'nor's advice on an embarrassing situation – one which could lead to lack of proper co-operation between his sub officer and a leading firefighter.'

'You wouldn't do that.'

'That's exactly what I'll do if you don't get in.'

Pearce got in.

He stared sullenly ahead as Hallam said: 'Look, this is all about Patti, isn't it? Now, I don't know what sort of picture she's been giving you, but I can tell you there's nothing in it. So you can stop treating me like a suspect, all right? On duty or off.'

'That's what I'm doing, is it?' grunted Pearce. 'I thought I was making it easier, keeping it private, that's all.'

'What, stalking off all ruffled up to the bus stop in front of half the Watch? They're not daft.' In his mirror Hallam saw a bus looming up behind him, and drove off. 'They'll be dreaming up some lovely ideas right now if I don't put a stop to it.'

'And how are you going to do that? Tell them all my wife's a tart? They'd love that, wouldn't they? Then what do I do – transfer again, like last time?'

'Like last time?' Hallam echoed. 'Look, Geoff, what is all this?' When Pearce again went mum, Hallam swerved the car into a side street and stopped. 'Come on.'

Miserably, yet with a certain relief, Pearce said: 'Why d'you think I came to Blackwall in the first place?'

'Hoping to get some metropolitan experience. Then maybe back to Bristol with qualifications under your belt, and an offer of promotion.'

'Back to Bristol?' Pearce shuddered. 'That's one place I can't set foot in again. We had to leave. It was her fault.'

He was looking at Hallam almost as dodgily as Patti had looked at him when they first met. Hallam wondered how much Pearce knew – or guessed – about that stupid incident in his own house; or how much Patti had told him, embroidering as she went along.

There was no holding Pearce now. The sombre surroundings were drawing him out, the way a haunted house might draw out non-stop talk to cover eerie silences or uncomfortable sounds. 'There was a Brigade do,' he went on. 'A big social occasion: leaving party for one of the lads. A lot of drink going the rounds, you know. Patti was talking to the guv'nor and his wife, and then he went out and she must have slipped out after him. Later that night . . .' Pearce swallowed, but was determined to go on. 'In bed that night, she told me the guv'nor had made a pass at her, and what was I going to do about it?'

'Awkward,' said Hallam inadequately.

'Yes. As it turned out, she was lying. She'd made a pass at *him*.'

Why the hell was Pearce telling him all this? Wanting to draw him out and confirm that something like this had happened that evening when the lights went out?

'In the end, I thought it wasn't worth making a fuss. One way or the other, it wasn't worth it. I wasn't really . . . well, not really angry enough. I suppose I ought to have been. But not enough to damage my career.' Pearce looked out into the pallor of the evening. 'She always wants what she can't have.'

Maybe that was the lot. He had got it off his chest, and there wouldn't be any awkward questions left for the sub to cope with. Hallam said, as casually as possible: 'Well, that's all behind you.'

'Yes. Has to be, hasn't it? Only, the guv'nor

couldn't stop himself telling it to someone in the club one night. It got round the station. Then the whole division. You can guess how it went. The sub's missis is easy meat. Raring for it. Silences, comments, giggles. You know what it can be like.'

'Oh, a few drinks, we all get silly now and then.'

'That's what I told myself. Put it down to the drink. But,' said Pearce intensely, 'I don't think it's as simple as that. She's always been . . . odd. Maybe if we'd had a kid and . . . but no. She gets squeamish. You know, when I helped that woman in that crash to give birth, I told Patti about it, and how suddenly there was this little boy – you know, cord and everything – and I'd been the one who delivered it. And she looked so disgusted. Didn't know how I could have done it, and didn't want to hear about it.'

'Phew. I'd no idea.'

'I didn't want anyone to have any idea. But now that it's starting up all over again – '

'Nothing's starting up,' said Hallam vehemently. 'Whatever happened last time in Bristol, or any other time, Patti didn't get past square one with me. Is that clear? As far as I'm concerned, it never happened and I don't want it happening ever. Get that into your head. And try and get it into Patti's head too, because if Sandra gets any . . .' He slammed his hand down on the steering wheel. 'Oh, God.'

'What?'

'Sandra. I said I'd drive straight home this evening and take her in to her class. It's the last one before she tries this new job she's got lined up.'

He did a screeching three-point turn that would have won him approval during a driving test if it had not been for the noise, and raced back towards the junction.

Pinned to the front door was a scrawled message which said simply: *Thanks a lot!*

Nick was thankful for a quiet beginning to the first evening watch since young Donald's death. He made sure of the routine paperwork, checking every page of the attendance register, going through equipment records and copies of the last week's reports to H.Q., especially that on the death, and trying to outguess Scase on any awkward questions. With all that out of the way, he could spare some time for swotting up on his A.D.O. interview. It was essential to be systematic. He had indexed all the likely interview subjects on file cards: fires, flooding, special services, training resources, equal ops. He couldn't write a complete crib on his sleeve: everything had to be memorized.

The flow of this thought was broken into by one telephone call. He had told Ariadne not to call him at Blackwall, but she seemed incapable of letting him detach himself entirely from her for an unbroken fifteen hours. She kept it short, willing to release him if he agreed to a time and a place she had already worked out. If he argued, the call was bound to be a protracted one.

He agreed, and then tried to force his mind back to a recitation of the official chain of command, which took priority in exams over such humdrum matters as floods, fires, and the release of trapped motorists from crumpled vehicles.

It was growing dark when he was summoned to a black limousine parked in the shadows of the yard. As he approached, a uniformed Brigade driver got out and opened the rear passenger door, then wandered a few discreet paces down the road to light a cigarette. Commander Bulstrode was waiting inside, his dinner jacket adorned with medals.

'This won't take long, Georgiadis. I'm going to a dinner tonight. Top brass. Might learn a thing or two about all our futures. And I expect there'll be a few derogatory remarks about letting that young dimwit slip off the roof.'

'Sir, with respect – '

'You know' – the A.C.O. ploughed on – 'I don't envy you, being in the front line. Used to, when I got made up to Staff. For years I secretly hankered to be back on the run. But not any more. It's a different Brigade to the one I joined, and it's changing by the minute.'

Nick, looking out into the dusk, wondered what was coming next.

'This little fellow Scase. Has he been around at all?'

'A couple of times. A turn-out drill, paperwork investigation. There's a feeling he'll be springing a surprise station visit on us.'

'I'm sure he will. Seems to be waging a holy war against this division, and Blackwall in particular.'

'I can't think why, sir. I mean, I gather he had a bit of a run-in with my predecessor, but – '

'More to it than that. I'll tell you why. But this is to go no further. Understood?'

Nick nodded.

'It's me they're after. And they're using Scase and Blackwall to do it.'

'Who's "they"?'

'Some sort of cabal at H.Q. Middle ranks. Those who regard me and my generation as dinosaurs. They're ambitious men, and they want to force me out. They see themselves as the future. Blackwall's one of the sticks they'll beat me with when the time comes. When this place was up for closure, I fought long and hard for it behind the scenes. Oh, yes, it was me who kept you open. And you never had a clue how close the chop was getting, did you?'

Nick thought of Scase's undisguised sneers. 'There've been one or two hints, sir.'

'Have there, now? Anyway, I put my neck on the line for Blackwall and other stations like it because I believed in what the rest of them call an old-fashioned type of station. And now they're looking for any way to discredit it: the way it's run, response times, the building itself, so they can hold it up as an example of an old man's folly. That's what Scase is up to.'

'With respect, sir, I don't see what I can do. I mean, I appreciate your telling me all this, but – '

'I'm telling you so that you can be on your guard. Don't give him anything to use against you. I know things didn't work out between you and my daughter, but that aside, I think highly of you. You're good at your job. The Brigade's going to need people like you once the management consultancy boys get busy.' Wearily he rubbed his eyes. 'You know, the irony of all this is that I'd been intending to retire this year anyway. You, on the other hand, are up for promotion. You're doing the right thing. Move up and out. Because Blackwall may not exist in a year's time.' He sank into brooding silence, and that seemed to be the end of it until he sighed and concluded: 'That's about it, Georgiadis. Watch your back. And watch Scase.'

'A bit difficult doing both at once,' Nick ventured, 'if he creeps up behind me.'

'Oh, he'll creep all right. You'll have to devise your own rear-view mirror.'

Bulstrode's visit proved a timely one. Blue Watch had been on its next day shift for little more than five minutes when a Brigade car turned into the yard. Pearce spotted it and fussed forward, but

D.O. Scase, getting out, ignored him and strode towards the station.

Nick came down the stairs. 'Good morning, sir.'

'Just passing, Georgiadis. Thought I'd check everything was shipshape.'

'You'd like the inspect the station?'

'Indeed.'

Nick smiled respectfully. Thanks to Bulstrode's warning, he had set the Watch to clearing the whole place out from top to bottom. Even the accumulation of old material and uniforms in the loft had been tidied up.

He deferentially stood aside as Scase began pacing around, peering into corners and fingering doors in the locker room like a Victorian housewife checking that the maid had not skimped on the dusting. The station officer's unconcern ruffled Scase, but he kept his lips tightly shut, storing up energy for the moment when there was something to criticize.

They were in the general office when the bells went down.

'Fire in a container lorry on the Woolwich ferry, guv.'

Nick was reluctant to leave Scase snooping about on his own – not because he felt the Watch might have overlooked something, but because he could not be sure that the man wouldn't plant something when nobody was looking. That was hardly an objection you could raise with a superior officer. He said politely: 'You'll be all right, sir?'

'Quite happy, thank you. Off you go.'

When they returned from the blaze on the ferry deck, Scase was just emerging from the station and heading for his car.

'My compliments, Mr Georgiadis. A very neat station.' He could hardly conceal his disappointment.

'You seem surprised, sir.'

'Not in the least. Cleanliness is next to godliness, and I commend you. Though I find your cook a trifle surly.'

Nick wondered what Maggie had said to the prowling visitor; or, more likely, what she had stonily not said.

He watched as Scase's car drove off the premises, just in case some second malicious thought brought the D.O. back in again. When he was satisfied that the coast was clear, he got his revision papers out again and spent most of the morning and afternoon without interruption except for a brief spell dealing with a routine kitchen fire.

That evening he went home with the papers in his brief-case, all set for a couple more hours, this time accompanied by half a bottle of wine. Getting out of his car, he locked the doors and walked towards the doorway of the block of flats.

'Nick.'

He turned to find a hunched, stocky shape

a few feet away. 'Yanni. What are you doing here?'

'Waiting for you, of course.'

There was a dull menace in it that made Nick glance around to see if any of Yanni's heavies were in the background. He was often accompanied by large men who were referred to obliquely as personal assistants. This evening he seemed to be alone.

'Do you want to come in?'

'What I have to say is better said outside. On neutral ground.'

'Really?'

'Yes, really. I don't know if you're aware, but I paid for Ariadne's honeymoon. For my goddaughter – that was my gift to them.'

'Generous of you. A nice thought.'

'I don't know how much they enjoyed it. I had hoped it would be a lot. But of course I was sent the hotel bill for settlement. It listed a number of phone calls to London. Most of them to you, Nick. And on their return, while her husband was spending a few hours with his sick mother, Ariadne told him she would go to see a girlfriend. But she came straight round here. Don't bother to deny it. I was here. I saw her. And that was only the first time.'

At least this gave Nick a chance to work up some indignation before the accusations got any worse. 'You've been following her?'

'Nick, you have been incredibly indiscreet. Let

me tell you this. Ariadne is my goddaughter. I will not see her shamed and her marriage made a mockery.'

'Yanni, I think you've misunderstood – '

'I have misunderstood nothing. Nick, I've known you since you were a boy. I knew your parents, even your grandparents. And there was a time when I believed – we all did – that you and Ariadne were made for each other. But you chose to move away from that. And now, when she is married, you think it is all right to move back again?' His narrow, vulpine head stabbed forward under the street light. 'If you come near Ariadne again, if you even try to touch her, if you even speak her name . . . so help me, I will kill you.'

Giving Nick no chance to stutter out any sort of reply, Yanni turned and walked off.

15

There was an hour to go before stand-down. Jaffa Parrish of Red Watch had arrived early, as promised, and was changing as George hurried up the stairs to tap on the station officer's door.

'Guv, is it all right if Jaffa Parrish rides for me? Just for an hour, he'll really only be on standby. He's in early, and I wouldn't mind getting away.'

Georgiadis raised a cynical eyebrow. He was obviously wondering what line of moonlighting George was into at the moment. 'Is he ready?'

'Just changing, guv. I've asked him, and he doesn't mind.'

'Make sure he's booked before you leave.'

'Sure.'

George was at the door when Georgiadis said: 'Oh, and George . . .'

'Yes, guv?'

'Don't drop any pianos, will you?'

'No, guv.'

George grinned ruefully. That was just what Jaffa had said too.

His pace quickened as he turned down the alley towards the stage door. It was a drab stretch of paving which by the end of the evening would be littered with empty beer bottles and cans, but he had come to regard it as an entry to wonderland.

Tommy was ready with the keys for his first task of unlocking the fire exit doors. 'Feller in charge says thanks for coming in early. They've got to rehearse, so he appreciates it. You're making a big impression, they've all been singing your praises.'

'All?'

'Well, specially that little Larissa. Asking if you was around. Wish I was your age again.' Tommy wiped a rheumy eye. 'Been some lovely girls here, George. I've seen some lovely girls.'

'So you've told me.'

George moved on. He paused in the wings, seeing the dancers sweeping across the stage in a flurry of movement from which Larissa emerged, poised for a moment of utter stillness on her toes, and then flew round the back of the group on invisible wings. She caught his eye; smiled a ravishing smile; and seemed to take new strength from his awestruck, answering smile.

The ballet season would soon be over. She would

soon be gone. The music from the orchestra pit sounded more melancholy than ever.

By fifteen minutes to six the two men in the cylinder depot yard had decided to pack it in for the day. There had been two deliveries of fully charged gas cylinders while they were still trying to stack empties ready for refilling, and they were tired of heaving the things around. Reorganization could wait until the morning.

The yard was a large open area with a high brick wall at one side and a wire mesh fence along the other, hemmed in by houses. It had been a builder's yard, but was now subdivided into storage areas unevenly enclosed by leaning lengths of corrugated sheeting, each section jammed with clusters of propane gas cylinders, overlooked by the manager's portakabin.

Glancing at his watch, Clive Evans shoved and kicked a stray cylinder impatiently over the potholes and rutted ground to prop it against a section of sheeting.

Bob, the manager, finished locking a flat-bed truck and called across: 'Oy, go a bit easy, will ya?'

'Nothing in them, is there?'

'Empty vessels make the most noise, right? So keep it down.'

Bob headed for the office as Clive settled his crash helmet on his head and pulled his motor-bike away from the wall of the portakabin. Inside, Bob looked out of the window to wave a perfunctory goodbye, and at the last moment saw a white frost of leaking propane from the stray cylinder. Before he could shout, Clive's foot jabbed into a kick-start.

There was a deafening thunderclap. A balloon of flame expanded from the leaking cylinder. Shock waves blew the glass window to pieces as Bob ducked down in terror. He clawed his way up again in time to see the fuel tank of the bike explode. Another cylinder detonated like a bomb as flames engulfed it, and the air was filled with flying shrapnel.

Bob lugged the extinguisher from the office wall and headed out. Another cylinder suddenly went up in a fireball and blasted him under the truck. A pall of smoke and flames surrounded him in a theatrical funeral pyre.

At Brigade headquarters control room, the peace of the late afternoon began to hot up. The call light glowed red beside the information board. In calm routine an operator switched into the call. Within a matter of seconds the red light demanded another response; and another. The watch commander began to realize that they could have a major incident on their hands.

'Fire and explosion in storage yard, Faro Road.'

And in Blackwall, the closest station to the incident, the machine began to reel out its commands. 'Fire and explosion, Faro Road.'

'That's not where George has gone a-moonlighting,

is it?' said Jaffa. 'You know he's not safe out on his own.'

They set out in good spirits. It was only as the leading appliance approached the street beside the yard that the full enormity of it hit them. Leaping spirals of smoke were nothing out of the ordinary. But the lethal, fiery missiles which ripped their way over and through the roofs of neighbouring houses were a rare hazard. As the pump ladder did a difficult slalom between miniature bonfires in the tarmac, a flaming cylinder screeched a few yards ahead of them and scorched its way into the front garden of a house. Chunks of metal rained into the street. Two top storeys of semi-detached houses burst into flames.

Nick Georgiadis assessed the situation as the pump and pump ladder moved towards the depot. There were people trapped on the first floor of one blazing house. He began ordering Hallam to take his crew and work their way along the back to evacuate everyone out of harm's way. It was easier said than done. The cylinders were launching themselves from the yard like World War II flying bombs in murderous parabolas. Prickling with apprehension against the next onslaught, Georgiadis closed in on the pump, with Jaffa at the wheel.

'Take the pump down the far end. We'll work our way down to you.'

Jaffa drove off as the rest of the crew followed

the station officer towards the gates of the depot. They had hardly stepped off the street on to the depot approach when another cylinder rushed down on to a parked car. The whole lot went up in a fury of fire. There seemed to be no hope of doing anything about the depot itself without a hefty back-up.

Through the inferno it was just possible to glimpse Jaffa getting down from the pump and arguing with an elderly lady determined to fight off any idea of leaving her home. As two more appliances rolled up in support, Georgiadis hurried Sally Reid and Billy Ray along the front of the houses.

'She won't move without her blasted cat,' yelled Jaffa as the three of them approached.

'Leave that. Get on the radio. Make pumps twelve.'

'Right, guv.'

Jaffa was climbing into the cab and reaching for the handset when a massive explosion erupted behind the nearest houses. A burning cylinder ploughed through a flimsy garden fence and came straight towards the appliance.

Georgiadis and the nearest members of Blue Watch stared in disbelief as the cab erupted and, as the tanks went up, the pump disappeared within a vast, swelling curtain of flame.

The three of them dragged themselves from their trance of horror and raced round the bonnet of the blazing pump, expecting to find only a charred corpse. But Jaffa had been blown clear of the cab on to the road. Pearce and Recall pulled him away, whimpering, while Georgiadis turned to bellow up the road: 'Kevin, get an ambulance up here quick.'

He was gazing into an apocalyptic nightmare. Cars parked down one side of the road were on fire, and two houses were beginning to blaze. Fire, police and ambulance personnel were making their way round from a side road; but it would be a chancy business for them to get any closer to the Blackwall pump at the heart of the blaze.

A Brigade control vehicle pulled to a halt at the far end of the cylinder depot. Through drifts of smoke, the Blue Watch team could glimpse D.O. Scase donning his gear at the rear of the Land Rover.

As gently and tenderly as possible, Pearce and Recall were carrying the slumped form of Jaffa Parrish to the shallow protection of a front garden wall.

Nick gasped into his Evac: 'Echo two zero zero, from Blackwall Pump One. Priority. One firefighter suffering burns. Request attendance air ambulance at fireground. Over.'

An appliance was making a dash through the intermittent barrage. As the newcomers jumped down, Nick wordlessly directed them to tackle the blazing pump, which was effectively sealing off the road.

Recall bent over the charred, hideous face of Jaffa, making soothing noises that made no sense.

An invalid was being carried from a house which was beginning to burn forwards and outwards from an attack like that of a flame-thrower against the rear wall.

In Brigade headquarters control room, all the consoles were manned as the scale of the outbreak became clearer. D.O. Scase had just made pumps fifteen. One appliance had been reported burnt out, one firefighter seriously injured; and more calls for ambulances to collect people moved out of their houses, some in shock, some scorched by flying debris. Mass evacuation of the whole area was under way.

News crews and cameras were closing in, obstructing the streets, taking stupid risks, and asking stupid questions to which nobody had the time or ability to reply.

D.O. Scase reached Nick Georgiadis. 'What's your situation here?'

'We've spotted a person trapped, sir, under a truck in the yard. Sub Officer Hallam and a crew are trying to find a way in. Parts of the wall have gone and they think they can get through.'

'Let's hope they're right. Anyway, you look after

this sector and we'll get support in the other side. Carry on, Georgiadis.'

'I've still got one of my crew injured on the fireground, sir. Any word on the air ambulance?'

'Yes,' said Scase briskly, 'I've stopped that. The medics are just up the road. They'll get him out as fast as they can.'

'You did what? That man was seriously burnt. I asked for him to be airlifted.'

'That's right. You did. And I stopped it. Those things are going up like Exocet missiles – you think I'm going to risk a bloody helicopter coming in?' Before Nick could protest again, Scase said: 'You're not the officer in charge here, Georgiadis. I am. You stick to my decisions, all right?'

Scase stamped away. Nick's rage had to be directed elsewhere as another cylinder hurtled past him and destroyed a trim little front garden. Pearce and Recall were helping the paramedics to stretcher Jaffa with infinite care into the lee of an abandoned double-decker bus to wait for an ambulance, apparently oblivious to their own danger from fiery shrapnel. As Nick passed them, Pearce said: 'He'd still be in his own Watch at the station, any other day. Not going to make George feel too good, is it?' It was an obvious truth; but only Poison Pearce would have spoken it out loud.

As he reached the yard wall, Nick saw Hallam and Sicknote crouching close to a gap which had been blown through the brickwork. They were overlooked by an evacuated house, with a Shadbrook hose crew at the window getting their hoses into position.

'He's wedged under that rear wheel,' said Hallam. 'Too close to the petrol tank for comfort. Sure you're ready for this?'

'Can't wait,' said Sicknote between clenched teeth.

Hallam looked up once more at the hose crew and gave them the thumbs up. Two jets of water sprayed the yard at full power as the two Blue Watch men launched themselves out into the open. Sprayed by the deluge from above, they made for what was left of the hut, circling away from the still exploding arsenal of gas cylinders and keeping their heads well down until they could crouch down again, this time within the remnants of the portakabin. Hallam paused, counted three for no good reason, and made a break for the motionless figure lying by the truck. Before he could reach it, a deafening blast through the clouds of smoke blew him off his feet and rolled him over twice, out into the battlefield of the yard. Sicknote sprang towards him, got him upright again, and rushed him back into their flimsy cover.

The fierce watery arcs of the hoses slashed their curtain back across the ground. Hallam counted up to three again; and he and Sicknote made another dash. This time they got to the depot boss, dragged him clear of the truck, and carried him back the way they had come, occasionally holding up their heads in gratitude for the drenching they were getting. They got a last pummelling thrust on their way as the truck exploded behind them.

'Well done, the pair of you.' Nick ducked as a huge fireball erupted from the fuel tank. He glanced wryly at Hallam. 'Your bright idea, was it?'

It was Sicknote who replied. 'Don't blame me guv, it certainly wasn't mine.' He sagged back against what was left of the wall. 'I'm soaking. We'll be lucky if we don't get pneumonia in this state.'

Hallam summoned up the strength to speak. 'No chance. Too warm, isn't it?'

D.O. Scase was bustling about in the background. Nick made a wide circuit to avoid him, anxious to check on Bayleaf and others who were still shepherding dazed people out of their homes. It always amazed him how many folk, threatened with death by smoke and fire within a matter of minutes, could still argue about leaving and complain that they needed time to collect the cat, their video recorder, or the contents of the refrigerator. So many of them managed to be terrified and yet stubborn at the same time.

It was another two hours before the chief officer, who had arrived on the scene closely behind D.O. Scase, was prepared to declare the area safe. It made a devastating sight. Over half the neighbouring houses looked as if they had been subjected to constant bombardment during a no-holds-barred battle course. Within what was left of the contours of the yard there were huge craters, littered by splinters and bricks like a huge fall of autumn leaves. The smoke was wispy now, but its stench carried for miles over the streets of the district.

Nick, almost dead on his feet, stumbled towards Scase.

'I'd like a word before we go, sir. About my order you stopped, for Parrish.'

Scase wiped the back of his hand across his mouth, leaving a dark smear, and said with some relish: 'Still rankling, is it? Put it in your report, if you want it on record, Georgiadis. I can live with that, don't worry.'

'I'll do that, sir,' said Nick evenly. 'I'll also report that it wasn't a safe situation for a helicopter rescue. I should have considered that as well as worrying about Parrish. I was wrong. Goodnight, sir.'

He had meant it as a direct, honest admission. But he was none too displeased by the fact that it had left Scase, for once, completely nonplussed.

The orchestra was working up to a fine fortissimo climax as it approached the interval, and the dancers swirled into a dizzying ensemble around Larissa, held high by her partner after their *pas de deux*. Applause rolled up over the stage before the echoes of the final chord had died away.

George nodded at old Tommy in his cubicle. 'Lapping it up out there, eh?'

'Been a fair old show for you lot tonight, too.' Tommy gestured towards his portable radio. 'Quite a news flash, that was.'

'How's that?'

'Bottled gas depot went up, Blackwall. Stuff flying about like the blitz. Got half the fire engines in the business there, by the sound of it.'

A chill ran down George's spine. 'All right if I use your phone?'

He was answered by Suffolk, station officer of the duty Watch, in snappish mood. Yes, the news reports were true. And he was seething because Blue Watch had gone out before Red Watch took over, and they had no other Blackwall appliances to carry them to the scene and lend a hand. Yes, someone had copped it: so far they didn't know quite how badly, but he ought to be on his way to hospital right now.

'Who was it?' George conjured up a visible roll-call of Bayleaf, Sicknote, Kevin and the rest of them.

'Hold it a minute. They're coming in.'

Suffolk kept him hanging on for a minute as the pump ladder rolled into the bay, followed by a Brigade personnel vehicle carrying the crew of the destroyed pump. Better for a Blue Watch eye-witness to tell George the details.

It was Recall who came to the phone. George

listened, disbelieving, with the chill spreading through his whole body until he began shivering uncontrollably. 'Jaffa? No.' He kept saying it: 'No . . .no . . . not Jaffa . . .'

Jaffa, in his place. It was impossible. But Recall wouldn't be making it up. Impossible but true. Jaffa, where George himself ought to have been.

'Where is he? Where've they taken him?'

'George, he's in good hands.'

'Where, for Christ's sake?'

'The burns unit at St Clothilde's. But they won't let you see him, George. Not yet.'

George heard that, but in his daze of horror refused to take it in. He had to get to Jaffa, see him, say something: somehow turn back the clock and make everything all right again.

Recall was saying, 'George, it could have been any of us, it's one of those things that happens, and it's happened, and nobody could have foreseen it,' as George hung up and went down the corridor for a quick word with Tommy. He passed Larissa coming offstage, flushed and triumphant and waiting for him to look at her and answer her smile. He went past her and out into the evening.

At first the staff nurse on duty refused to let him anywhere near the patient. Rules were rules. The patient's family were there, and that was it. She eyed George with some concern as his fists clenched. It was true he felt like pushing her out of the way and marching on towards the window of the room where Jaffa's wife and two others were peering wretchedly in. Then he spotted a Brigade divisional officer near them, quietly ready to offer counsel.

'Sir. Firefighter Green, Blackwall. That man in there was riding for me, sir. I've got to see him.'

'I think we have to fall in with hospital regulations, Green.'

'But sir, that should have been me. I've got to see him,' George implored again.

The D.O. glanced at the nurse, who relented. She led the way to the window, beside Jaffa's wife. Jaffa himself was on a ventilator, eyes closed and almost obscured by the scorched, puffy skin around them. A raw redness shading to purple covered the peeled horror of the rest of his face.

'The burns are still swelling,' the staff nurse explained in an undertone, though there was no way she could have disturbed the patient. 'His throat's blocked. He'll be more comfortable in a few days.'

Without daring to look at Jaffa's wife, George said: 'I'm sorry, Mrs Parrish. I wish it was me, I really do.'

She shook her head sympathetically, but could not find any words to say.

He got back to the theatre in time for the last half hour of the performance. He could not bear to look at the brightness of the stage or the grace of the movements there. All the brightness had been blacked out, so far as he was concerned.

When the audience had gone and the performers were packing up ready to leave, he began plodding mechanically through his safety procedure. Tommy, eager to pump him for melodramatic news, had taken one look at his face and for once succeeded in keeping his voice under wraps. It was only as he went to the front of the house that George spoke; and then only because Larissa was there, waiting for him, concerned for him.

He explained to her. All at once he had to talk, go over it all again. Half of him was still haunting that hospital window, looking: that was all he could do. It wasn't just the injuries: he had seen plenty of those before, and worse. It was knowing that it should have been him and not Jaffa. It was his fault that Jaffa was lying there like that.

Larissa laid her long, delicate fingers over his hand. 'No, George. Was not fault of yours. Was bad to happen, but was very big fire, yes? Terrible. But fire was not fault of yours.'

George nodded, uncomforted. He could tell himself that and would go on telling himself that, and he knew that when he got back to Blackwall the rest of the Watch would tell him that, just as Recall had already tried to do. It wouldn't do either Jaffa or himself any good.

16

News from the hospital in the morning seemed reasonably promising. Jaffa was still on a ventilator, but they thought he was holding up. Bayleaf went back to the breakfast table, where the front page of the morning paper featured a blurred picture of smoke and burning vehicles. Captured in still life, it lacked the uproar and heat of reality.

'Apparently George turned up at the ward last night, in a right state.' He realized Clare was not listening, but had put a couple of letters on the table between them. 'Post's early today, isn't it?'

'These are from yesterday. I didn't want to show you them last night. You'd had enough for one day. But I think you'd better have a look now. They're from the restaurant.'

'You mean they've been forwarded?'

'No. I brought them back with me. I went down there yesterday, after we got a snotty letter from Mr Bridges. Just after you'd left for duty.'

'Bridges – the builder? What's he been doing?'

'Nothing. Except writing to complain about a cheque bouncing, and getting no joy from our partner, Mr Grove. Nobody seems to be doing much at all, apart from the postman.'

'Hold it a minute. What's this about you going down there? You never said.'

'I've already told you. The state you were in when you got back last night, I thought it'd better wait. Only we better not wait too long.'

'All right, let's have it.'

Clare let him have it.

The aggressive letter from the builder had got her worried about the whole project again. She tried ringing Trevor's office, but was fobbed off by a weary-voiced girl who said Mr Grove was out but she would get him to ring back. By noon nobody had rung, and when Clare tried again the phone went on ringing without anybody answering. She could drive to Littlehampton and back before the kids came home from school, but left a note for Melanie just in case she was late.

The exterior of the restaurant looked just as shabby as when they had first seen it. No progress appeared to have been made on smartening it up. An old pick-up truck on the muddy forecourt was half loaded with debris. But at least there was some sound of activity inside.

A young pony-tailed labourer was carting away old wood and shreds of carpet underlay from the gutted area.

Clare said: 'Hello. Who are you?'

'Me? Chris. What's it to you?'

'I'm a partner in this business. We're anxious to know when the job'll be finished.'

'As far as we're concerned, it's finished.'

'But . . .' Clare gestured helplessly at the shambles all around them.

'Look, all I know is Mr Bridges told me to clear up what we done and leave it. We ain't had no money for a fortnight, and there's no materials come in.'

'And Mr Grove hasn't been here to . . . well, sort it out?'

'The geezer with the big motor? Saw him when we started, that was it.' He studied her, and liked what he saw well enough to ease off. 'You're the Wilson bit of it, are you? Grove and Wilson?'

'Yes – me and my husband. He's at work. I'm just trying to find out what's going on here.'

'Yeah, so's Mr Bridges.' Chris waved to a corner table just inside the entrance. 'There's a pile of mail over there, that might help. You may as well take it when you leave – nobody else will.'

Clare picked up the envelopes, nearly all of them brown and too many of them from the Inland Revenue and H.M. Customs and Excise. Now she splayed them out on the table in front of

Bayleaf, open, and let him read what she had already read.

At last he said: 'But Trevor should have paid all this lot right away. The money was there.'

'Our money,' said Clare dismally.

'Oh, there must be some explanation. We're new to this game, I'm sure we'll find – '

'Personally,' said Clare, 'I'd like to find Trevor and have it out with him.'

Bayleaf shuffled the demands together again as if to try a new deal which would come right this time.

'I'll ring his office.'

'I wish you joy.'

He tried ringing. Nobody answered. 'It's a bit early in the day. These types don't roll up until mid-morning.' Even in his own ears the attempted excuses sounded pretty feeble. He tried Trevor's home number; and got only an answering machine. He left a message, while Clare watched him fatalistically. 'Tell you what, I'll go round there myself.' As much as anything he wanted to yank her out of her creeping depression. 'We'll sort this out. Look, if it gets late, I'll go straight on duty this evening. All right?'

She was staring at her cup of tea, gone cold by now. 'Sure. Call me if you do.'

Bayleaf felt his optimism had been vindicated when he found the office door open, though the welcome was none too warm. The secretary in the constricted outer office had a petulant little mouth, very red in a sallow complexion, repelling rather than inviting. Whatever capabilities she had as a secretary, she had clearly had no training as a receptionist. She did not utter a word or look even vaguely interested in Bayleaf's presence until he said: 'I'm looking for Trevor Grove.'

'He hasn't been here for days.' Her voice was as constricted as the office itself.

'I've already gathered he hasn't been showing up here for days. My wife has tried ringing him, and I've tried this morning and tried his house.'

'There you are, then.'

'Yes, but where's *he*?'

'Mr Grove is out of town. He's unavailable. Sorry.'

'Look, he's not at home, and he's not here. But he has to be somewhere. And what are you doing in his office if you don't know where he is?'

The girl picked up some files from the desk and made a pretence of riffling through them. 'I'm organizing company files. And I do happen to be busy.'

Bayleaf picked another file up from the desk. 'And what company would this be?'

'Do you mind?' She snatched it from him in an officious huff. 'That one's no longer trading. Mr Grove is in a new partnership. I'm working here on their behalf. Now just leave, will you?'

'No, I won't. And you're fired. Understood? Put that down and shove off.'

'I beg your pardon?'

'Mr Grove happens to be in partnership with me, sweetheart. See?' He took one of the O.H.M.S. envelopes from his inner pocket and waved it under her nose. 'Grove and Wilson, right? That's him . . . that's me. So you're working on my behalf, aren't you? And if I don't find out where he is, you're fired. How's that?'

Nothing could have made that pinched little face look other than sullen; but at least it was beginning to register a glimmer of concern.

'Look, I'm sorry. I thought you were another of those builders.'

It was not a remark to soothe Bayleaf's worries.

'Well, now that we've established who I am, perhaps you'll let me know precisely where Mr Grove is so that we can get together and sort out the business of those builders.'

The address was that of a caravan park five miles inland from Littlehampton. It was an attractive, wooded setting, but Bayleaf was in no mood to admire the scenery. He found the park, checked along the rows, and hammered on the door of Number 23.

He had half expected to find this, too, deserted. It was a surprise when the door opened to reveal Trevor.

It was obviously a surprise for Trevor, too. He

greeted Bayleaf with a momentary blench, then boomed out a welcome and began almost dragging him inside.

'Not exactly gracious living, Mike, but it's warm and dry. Used this quite a bit in my courting days. That used to steam it up.'

'Yeah, it would. So what are you doing hiding in it now?'

'I'm not hiding. Don't be daft. You found me, didn't you?'

'I had to work at it. What's that if it's not hiding?'

Trevor groped into the fridge and brought out two cans of lager, making a lot of noise slamming the door, slamming the cans boisterously down, opening them, and putting on an air of feigned reproach.

'Nothing of the sort. I'm still in touch. Got no choice for the moment. I can't go near the house, with the divorce going through.'

'You never told us about any divorce.'

'Didn't want to bore you. All the usual stuff. Preferred to concentrate on business – take the old mind off it, eh?'

'If you've been concentrating,' said Bayleaf, 'why couldn't you phone? You've got our number. We're supposed to be in business together.'

'Do you see a phone in here?' said Trevor plaintively.

Bayleaf decided to get down to the main matter

that had brought him here. He took out the sheaf of open brown envelopes and tipped the contents out one by one on the narrow work-top.

'What's all this about?'

Trevor plucked out the letters and bills, ran his eyes over them, then tossed them back on the work-top. 'Making work for penpushers, that's what. They're old returns, with a new name on. Not your problem. I send 'em back, they take it off. Simple as that. Leave 'em with me, all right?'

'But what about those builders? Why haven't they been paid properly?'

Trevor was beginning to relax. This all seemed to be familiar territory to him. 'Show me a builder who thinks he's been paid properly, and we'll hire him! I'll see that nit Willy tomorrow and tell him to put the cheque back in again. The money's sitting there waiting for him. He might get on with some work then, before the season hits us.'

'So where was the money when the cheque bounced?'

'In the bank, where it is now. I closed the old company account when we opened ours, but the cheque went in the old one. Their mistake, not mine. All he has to do is present it again. Or he can have cash, if he wants it. I don't mind.' Trevor grinned condescendingly. 'I can see his game, too. He's bitching at you because he knows he won't get away with it with me. I might not be on the phone here, Mike, but I'm on the ball. Don't fret about it.'

He prodded the lager can closer to Bayleaf. 'Want a sandwich while you're here?'

Bayleaf hesitated. But, after all, why not? It would have been a long way to come for nothing.

The inquest on Donald Graham Mabstock was held at the coroner's court fifteen minutes' walk from Blackwall Fire Station. Pearce, in undress uniform, was leaning against the corridor wall as his station officer arrived. The three benches in the corridor were all occupied.

'Shall we go and sit in there?' Nick nodded towards the waiting-room.

'Well, I . . . er . . . I think that's Donald's mother and sister in there. So I thought I'd wait here.'

Nick joined Pearce, leaning against the wall until they were called into the small courtroom.

The coroner's desk was at one end, with desks for a couple of agency reporters in front. A bench down one wall was reserved for the coroner's officer, with a police sergeant and a doctor beside him. In the centre of the room were several rows of benches for witnesses and the family of the deceased. A Brigade observer placed himself inconspicuously at the back.

'All rise for Her Majesty's Coroner.'

A woman in her late forties came in from a side door, crossed to her desk, and bowed to the court.

'Please sit,' intoned the coroner's officer.

The facts of Donald's background, including a medical report on his psychiatric problems, were tactfully drawn out. His mother, restraining her sobs, recalled his interest in fire engines and their crews, especially those of the nearby Blackwall station, and came close to breaking down when she gave details of his hideout in the upper floor of the old warehouse. Donald's sister, who often took a flask of coffee round when she knew he was playing there, described the models he had built, based on the fire station, complete with a matchwood appliance bay and toy engines. Cause of death was established by the doctor; and Station Officer Georgiadis was called to outline the Blackwall procedures that night which had led up to the death. He kept it brisk and impersonal, summing up the routine and the timing involved after the alarm was raised. Of the matter-of-fact questions raised by the coroner, there was only one he could not answer, because he had been directing firefighting operations at the front of the building, while Leading Firefighter Pearce and Firefighter Mackenzie went round to the rear fire escape.

It was Pearce's turn.

He started out in a deliberately dull recapitulation of the procedures the station officer had already covered, until the coroner courteously asked that he should present his evidence from the time when he and his colleague had gone to the rear of the building: from then on, they were the only ones in full possession of the relevant facts.

Pearce cleared his throat. 'When Firefighter Mackenzie and myself got to the back of the premises, we looked up and saw somebody on the fire escape. We recognized him as Donald, and called to him, but he ran further up, towards the roof.' He was trying to echo Nick's unemotional, purely explanatory tone. 'We pursued him – '

'Can I stop you there?' the coroner interrupted. 'Why did you need to – ah – *pursue* him?'

'Because he was in danger, and we needed to get him out of the burning building.'

'Yes, but, Leading Firefighter Pearce,' said the coroner patiently, 'we've heard from Donald's mother that he was devoted to the Fire Brigade and was a regular visitor at Blackwall Fire Station. He had come to think of you as his friends. Why should he run away from you?'

Pearce glanced uneasily at Nick, who allowed himself no flicker of response. 'I can only think, ma'am' – it came out slowly and tentatively – 'that he was scared. We learned afterwards that he must have started the fire as a game, but it got out of hand. He must've thought we'd be angry with him.' He paused, then tried again, forcing words out even more reluctantly. 'I suppose . . . he might also have been scared of me in particular, because . . . well, there was an earlier incident when I'd had to order him to leave the station.

I suppose I might have been a little heavy-handed in that.'

The coroner made a note. 'I see. Please continue.'

'Well, we went on to the roof and were calling his name out, but we couldn't see him. Then he suddenly appeared round a ventilation housing and saw us.'

There was a complete hush in the courtroom. It was all too obvious to everyone there that Pearce was re-living the whole experience, conjuring up an unforgettable vision before his eyes.

'He started to back away towards the edge of the roof. It all happened very quickly. I called to him again, and he went on backing away. He was calling for one of the other firefighters. He reached the parapet. I put my hand out to him, and then he stepped back on to some loose guttering. I tried to grab him. He fell backwards . . .' Pearce froze for a moment. The coroner made no move, giving him time to recover. 'Fell backwards,' Pearce repeated. 'And before I could catch him, he . . . he went over the edge. And fell into the courtyard below.'

The hush was broken by Mrs Mabstock's snuffles into a crumpled handkerchief.

'Thank you, Mr – ah – Leading Firefighter Pearce.'

While waiting for the summing-up and verdict, Pearce stood in the corridor some feet away from

Nick, incapable of saying another word, and keeping his distance from the two women with bowed heads in the waiting-room. Every minute of the interval seemed more and more ominous. When at last they were summoned back to the courtroom, Pearce went in like a man preparing to face a life sentence.

The coroner's face gave no hint of her final judgement. Looking down at her notes, she began: 'We have heard the medical evidence in this case, and from Station Officer Georgiadis the clear timetable of the firefighters' procedure on the night in question. I accept all this evidence and see no reason to sum it up again at this stage. The tragedy of this case, as I see it, is that Donald was afraid he had let down his friends from Blackwall Fire Station. That caused him in momentary panic to run away from them on to the roof, from where, sadly, he fell to his death.' She raised her head and looked directly at Pearce, who braced himself. 'The Fire Brigade,' she said firmly, 'acted in an exemplary fashion towards this young man; and, indeed, Leading Firefighter Pearce risked his own life trying to save him. I will therefore record upon the inquisition into the death of Donald Graham Mabstock that he died of head injuries sustained after falling from the roof of a disused factory in Apley Street, Blackwall, and I now record a verdict of misadventure.'

In the corridor outside, Nick was approached

by the Brigade observer for confirmation of two purely technical points. A few feet away he noticed Mrs Mabstock and her daughter, making no move towards the exit. Geoff Pearce, the last one to leave the courtroom, emerged to find himself right beside them. Nick tried to keep up the conversation with the man from H.Q. while straining to hear what trouble might blow up at this stage, and the possibility of a black mark going into the Brigade report.

'Excuse me, Mr Pearce.'

Pearce jolted to a halt. 'Er . . . yes?'

'We were just wondering,' said Mrs Mabstock, 'what exactly does that mean – misadventure?'

'It's like an accident.'

'That doesn't mean he was doing anything wrong?'

'No, no,' said Pearce awkwardly. 'Just that something he was doing *went* wrong . . . accidentally.'

'Good. Because he wasn't a bad boy, you know that. He just got confused by things. I don't know why he ran away from you that night. He loved all you lot. Apart from us, you were his only friends.'

The Brigade observer shook hands with Nick and strode away. Nick edged closer to Pearce and the two women.

Mrs Mabstock went on: 'I just wanted to say thank you for everything you did for him and for trying to save him.' She dug into her bag and took out a roll of paper. 'We found this in his room. I'm sure he'd have liked you to have it.'

Pearce took the paper with a trembling hand and unrolled it. It was a childish drawing in coloured pencil of the front of Blackwall Fire Station, complete with appliances and matchstick figures of the Blue Watch.

Another letter reporting a bounced cheque, this time for flocked wallpaper, had arrived.

'And why to our own address this time, after all the other stuff went to the Old Mill? They've tracked us down – or Trevor's been shifting the responsibility, lumbering us with all his other oversights?'

This time Clare overrode all Bayleaf's objections. No, she wouldn't wait for Trevor to come up with another plausible explanation. She was not going to waste any more time. They needed some impartial advice, and an old colleague of hers in the local welfare office had recommended a reliable accountant. It was high time they went to see him.

He was a Mr Philby of Philby, Foskett and Philby. Neither she nor Bayleaf ever learnt which specific Philby he was. He looked as cheerless as the surroundings of Littlehampton on a winter's day with drizzle blowing in off the Channel. Each bit of paper he turned over brought his jaw down another centimetre or so. At last he sucked his breath in through his teeth and said: 'Just how many cheques have been dishonoured before this little batch?'

'We don't know,' confessed Bayleaf. 'We've been leaving that side of it to Trevor, until we could decide when to move into the business full-time.'

'I see.' It was not a reassuring sound.

'We got to know about some problems, but I was told they'd been dealt with. Now there's this one, and plenty of final demands for unpaid invoices. Trevor was supposed to have cleared them all.'

Philby studied the papers. 'Trevor Grove. Mm. And this partnership was set up by Mr Grove's accountant, was it?'

'Yes.'

'Did you ever meet the gentleman?'

'Well, no.'

'Or introduce a representative of your own for a thorough discussion of mutual liabilities?'

Clare's head sank in utter dejection.

'No.' Bayleaf kept himself upright with an effort. 'Is the agreement invalid?'

'Not at all. It's perfectly legal. But I have to say that I think you have a problem.'

'Which is what?'

Mr Philby told them. Once they had become partners in an existing business, they became equally responsible for all its debts, unless they had agreed on an indemnity. Which, sadly, they had not. This meant that Mr and Mrs Wilson were personally responsible for all Mr Grove's bad debts. These amounted to a considerable sum. As to the bank account, in the last month Mr Grove had written cheques totalling over twenty thousand pounds – few of them connected with The Old Mill restaurant. Some debts had been cleared by these cheques, but there was nothing left in the account. In fact, the partnership was overdrawn by several hundred, which was why this last cheque had bounced.

'I suggest,' said Philby with the puritanical expression of one used to giving harsh advice to financial ignoramuses who deserved everything that came to them, 'that you both talk this thing through with Mr Grove and try to establish where the money you invested has gone.'

Clare raised her head to stare full at her husband. 'If he hasn't gone with it.'

17

There had been no word from Ariadne for three whole days. It was worrying; yet at the same time a relief. The intensity of it all had been taking his mind off his work. Leaving the station at the end of this day's watch, Nick could look forward to an uninterrupted evening with his manuals and notes. On the way home he dropped in at Uncle Dimitri's restaurant. He might as well make it a wholly carefree evening by avoiding any cooking for himself.

Dimitri came hurrying towards him. 'What you want?'

'Thought I might get a takeaway and a bottle of wine.'

'Is not possible.'

Nick looked around. It was early, and the restaurant did not appear particularly busy. 'Don't want a lot. Don't mind waiting a few minutes.'

'I told you, is not possible.'

'What d'you mean, it's not possible?'

'You know exactly what I mean. You bring shame to the family.'

'What have you been hearing?'

'Doesn't matter. I know it all.'

'Now wait a minute – '

'Nick. Don't make it more difficult, please. I have customers.'

'Not that many at the moment.'

'Makes no difference. No arguments, please.'

Nick looked into that implacable face, less powerful than Yanni's but just as hostile. 'Okay, uncle,' he said with taut, mock respect.

'And Nick – your motor-bike is still in Yanni's garage. He forgot to tell you he wants it taken away. I would advise you do so, before something happens to it.'

So much for a carefree evening. To get everything out of the way at one go, Nick drove his car home and then walked doggedly round to Yanni's house and rang the front doorbell.

Yanni said stonily: 'Oh, Nick. The shed door is unlocked. Perhaps you will let me have your spare key back. Right now.'

Nick handed over the key. 'I'll get the bike in a minute. But there's something I want to say first.'

'Nothing to say.'

'Listen, whatever ideas you've got about Ariadne and me, you haven't heard my side.'

'Nick, I don't want to know. Already I tell you: stay away. I should never even have let you use my premises in the first place. So take your bike and go.'

The front door was slammed shut.

Going round the side of house, Nick heard a tapping on an upstairs window. Ariadne was framed between the curtains, mouthing silently, helplessly at him. He tried to make out what she was trying to convey, but no sound came down through Yanni's expensive double glazing. He wanted to storm back to the front door and demand what they were doing to Ariadne: chaperoned, imprisoned, just as she had virtually been for most of the time before the wedding?

He got the bike out of the shed and rode home, finding a short stretch of pavement free from parked cars. By the time he had got indoors, there was a message on his answering machine.

'Nick, I heard what Yanni was saying to you at the door this evening. We have to talk. Do you know what they are trying to do to me? Ring me tomorrow – *please*. During the day, when Yanni is out. Petros has taken his mother back to Cyprus. And I think they plan for me to –'

The phone was cut off abruptly, either because Yanni had come upon her unawares or because Ariadne had heard him approaching.

In the morning he tried ringing. It was Yanni's

voice that answered. What was he doing home this time of day? Nick hung up.

Bayleaf brought morning tea in. 'Want anything to eat, guv?'

'No,' said Nick. As Bayleaf was on his way out he added: 'Close that door, will you?' And phoned again.

There was a long succession of rings, but this time no reply at all. Yanni must have gone out – and had he forced Ariadne to go with him?

Nick tried to turn his mind back to everyday routine. He went to the duty room, where Hallam was on the phone. At least Hallam had got someone communicating from the other end. 'What sort of potatoes? Yes, okay. No, we've got plenty of wine under the stairs, we don't need any more.'

'John, when you've finished your shopping list, I'm trying to run a fire station here.'

The next call was on the games room. Sicknote and Recall were not exercising but bent over a crossword puzzle on the window-ledge, arguing over a florid Shakespearean quotation. 'No, no, mate, if you knew your Richard the Third as well as I do . . . I mean, the number of times I've played that . . .' Sicknote's voice tailed away as Nick stepped forward.

'You finished all the roll-call assignments, Sicknote?'

'Yes, guv.'

'Well, actually you haven't. The bay's got some

oil stains on it. I want them cleaned off.' He saw the shock in their eyes. It wasn't like him. Well, they would learn just what he could be like. High time. When they glanced apprehensively at one another he said: 'Well, get moving.'

Prowling on, lashing out at random, he found Kevin in a corner of the mess. 'And you, Kevin.'

'I'm just finishing my tea break, guv. I'm not on the station cleaning detail today.'

'It's a hazard. It contravenes health and safety regulations. So you get out there and help clean it up. Now.'

He knew he was being unreasonable. And he was enjoying it. Or at least he was saving himself from thinking of other things.

On his next morning off he made his way to the nursery school as children came teeming out and heading along the pavement for their parents' cars. The supervisor was patting some on the head, steering a couple of recalcitrant girls away from the playground and towards the main gate, and waving graciously to a father standing by a Jaguar.

Nick said: 'Has Mrs Benaki finished for the day?'

'Ariadne?' The woman looked him up and down with a glint of curiosity. 'She hasn't been here since last weekend, I'm afraid. You're a . . . a friend of hers?'

'Yes. I hadn't heard from her for a while. I was just wondering. She's on holiday, or . . . ?'

'She just gave in her notice. Rather short notice. I got the feeling it must be personal, but she didn't say.' The woman was clearly a watchful type, used to sizing up children and their parents, and intuitive about other adults as well. 'You probably know more than I do, if she's a friend.'

The shock of discovering that Ariadne had simply left the part-time job which she had so much enjoyed, without letting him know – if she had even had an opportunity of letting him know – drove him round to Yanni's clothing warehouse to confront him yet again. He didn't know what he hoped to drag out of Yanni; didn't know why it had suddenly become more important than he could ever have dreamed; but knew that it was too late to be cautious, far too late to offer any pretences – least of all to himself.

Yanni was standing close to the exit from the loading bay, shaking hands with what looked like a prosperous customer. Not that Yanni himself ever looked less than prosperous. Nick waited for the customer to cross the road to his BMW, and then closed in.

'Where are they, Yanni? What's going on?'

He might not have been there. Yanni began walking towards the office door of the warehouse.

Nick seized his arm. 'I came here for an answer. You don't go till I get one.'

'Spiros.' One of the workmen at the loading bay called sharply to a burly figure at the end of the ramp. He took one look, jumped down, and began stomping towards his boss.

Yanni shook his head. Spiros pulled up, looked threateningly at Nick, and reluctantly turned back.

Nick's grip slackened. 'All right. But where is she?'

'You think you have the right to ask questions of me? What gives you the right? How many times must I tell you – '

'I can't get a word from her. Or from anywhere. She hasn't been to her job. Are you keeping her under lock and key?'

'A stupid notion. But none of it has anything to do with you, Nick.'

'Don't tell me you don't know what's going on.'

'I warned you,' said Yanni savagely. 'Both of you. But I saw this made no impression. On you or on her. So I ask myself what is to be done, if you are to be convinced.'

Nick was aware that although Spiros and the other men were steadily loading packages into a van, they missed no movement in the yard. But he was not going to be intimidated. 'You want to take it out on me,' he said, 'go ahead. Let your heavies loose. That won't change it.'

'Evidently. Or for her, I see that too. So I see that I must do something else. For Petros, for her own sake in the end. For this family.' Yanni was leaning forward, eye to eye. With slow, deadly emphasis he finished: 'Which is done. And no business of yours, Nick. You no longer belong to this family. Now go.'

Nick glared back at the men watching him. It was a feeling of futility rather than fear that turned him away. But he was going to have the last, adamant word.

'If Ariadne wants to be with me, you won't stop it, Yanni. You or any of you. I'll find her.'

It sounded fine, but what could it achieve? Just when he had learned how close he and Ariadne were, always had been and always ought to be, great distances had opened up between them. There was an emptiness inside him and all round him. *I'll find her.* But where did he start? The image of her was fleeing further and further away.

'A shame to see this season close, eh?'

'Especially as I'll be out of a job.'

'And you'll be sorry to see the dancers go home,' observed Tommy. When George made no reply, he added knowingly: 'You'll have to go out to Russia to visit her.'

'All right, Tommy, give it a rest.'

'There's another show opening here in a couple of weeks. I'm sure there'd be more work if you wanted it.'

George thought of the money, and Kelly wanting the money, but Kelly not wanting him to be out night after night. No: this was the final curtain so far as he was concerned.

Larissa came from her dressing-room, slim and fragile yet filling the whole world. No longer dressed in her tight blouse and tutu, her long, slender legs still seemed to go on forever, and those willowy arms still made movements that were pure music. She did not so much walk as float towards him.

'Can we talk?' Unaffectedly she took his hand and led him down to the auditorium. They sat in the centre of the front row of stalls. 'I brought you this.'

It was the programme for the ballet season, illustrated with photographs of the stars. Around the margins of one page were the autographs of the entire cast.

'Thanks.'

'Oh, George, you look so sad.' She touched his cheek. 'I too, I am sad. By this time tomorrow we are back in Russia.'

'Yeah, and I'm back in Blackwall.'

'Why do you not come and be a fireman in Saint Petersburg? We have big fires out there.'

'To make up for the one I missed here?'

'George, you still worry about your friend. Is not your fault.' Her hand strayed down his cheek to his neck, and she leaned forward to kiss him. 'This is my last night in London. I help you forget, yes? There is a bar at the hotel, it is open late, you come and be my guest and . . . how you say it . . . have "One for the street", yes?'

'I'd like to. But I've got to lock up, go through the safety procedures, and . . . go home.'

'George, I want you. Come back to the hotel with me.' The house lights were being methodically switched off. As they edged along the row of seats to the aisle, she said hungrily: 'George, you must come to me.'

He felt temptation stirring. It had been a day-dream for days now, taking on flesh each time he saw her. If there had been the chance last week, if Jaffa hadn't suffered such a staggering blow, if . . . Oh, there were so many ifs.

One of the dancers was calling urgently to Larissa from the wings, and a couple of musicians from the orchestra were urging her to hurry. George did not understand a word of the language, but the tone of voice was not hard to interpret. The atmosphere of a touring company obviously had a lot in common with the ribbing and insinuations within Blue Watch.

She kissed him again, and hurried away, with one backward glance of invitation.

Fifteen minutes later he checked the last fire door, padlocked the main fire exit, and made his way down the street to the corner in search of a taxi.

The hotel lights blazed out over the street more theatrically than the lights of the real theatre he had just left. He went slowly up the wide sweep of steps to the entrance. Beside it, the cocktail bar was a glitter of plate glass inviting the visitor to push through the swing doors and turn right.

Larissa, her deep auburn hair no longer austerely wound round her head but falling loose over her shoulders, sat toying with a tall glass, smiling wistfully to herself as she waited. She was so easily attainable now; yet so far away.

George watched for a long, long minute, as he had watched her in nightly enchantment on the stage. That was where she belonged: remote and untouched. He went slowly back to the pavement. He was a long way from home. Time to get going on the long haul back.

Uncle Dimitri came out of the restaurant, yawning and chatting in the doorway for a moment with the chef and one of his waitresses. As they said goodnight and left, he locked the door and was about to cross the street when Nick stepped forward and said: 'Where is she?'

Dimitri started. 'Nick, my God. What do you want at this time of night?'

'Where's Ariadne?'

Dimitri tried to walk round him, but Nick pressed closer, forcing him against the wall. Dimitri stumbled. He was made of less tough material than Yanni, and didn't have the back-up of Yanni's bruisers.

'She's not at your house or Yanni's, and she's not at their flat. She's given up her job – been *forced* to give it up, eh? Yanni won't tell me where she is, and the rest of you won't even speak to me.'

Dimitri was regaining his self-possession. 'Already I have told you. Why you keep on? You are surprised?'

'I'll tell you what I am. I'm sick of being treated like some sort of criminal. Sick of you and Yanni and all the others making moral judgements.'

'We have a right to – '

'You don't have any right. It's none of your business. Now: where *is* she?'

'Nick, it is the business of the family. You try to ruin a happy family. Don't make it worse. Stay away from them.'

Dimitri pushed himself away and began walking down the road. Nick followed him, furious. 'So Ariadne's happy, is she? That's why she rang me, and saw me, and why we – '

'Be quiet. I will not listen.'

'And if she's happy, why does she have to be hidden from me? You honestly think she's happy being married to Petros?'

'She wasn't forced to marry him. You had your chance, Nick. You rejected her.'

'Maybe I did, but things can change.'

'Too late. She's married.'

'But who to? Someone who treats her like a dog? Forces her to leave her job, so he can cart her back to his mother in Cyprus or something?'

He was suddenly sure. 'Is that where he's dragged her? To Cyprus?'

'Nick, please – '

'Wherever she is,' said Nick evenly, 'I'll find her.'

It sounded as resolute as it had sounded when he confronted Yanni.

In the morning, as he crossed the station yard, the echoes sounded a lot thinner. He could almost have prayed for a really dreadful incident that would take his mind off the frustrations of his own life.

Instead there was dull routine. Compton, Brigade training officer, arrived to give scheduled lessons on resuscitation, with Blue Watch one after the other giving the kiss of life sheepishly to an inflated dummy. It was a relief to the firefighters as much as to their station officer when the bells jangled a summons.

Kevin emerged from the watchroom. 'R.T.A., Blackwall Park Road.'

Few of their everyday call-outs could be described as pleasant, but this one proved particularly gruesome. They had to dismantle a car gingerly, bit by bit, around a trapped driver with a steel scaffolding pole right through his stomach, emerging from the middle of his back. He was alive when they sawed the ends of the pole off and handed him over to the paramedics; but none of them would have fancied being present when the pole was withdrawn.

Back in the station, Nick was on his way

up the stairs when Compton came out of the watchroom.

'Nick, I've just had a rumour on the blower. Some whisper of Bulstrode retiring.'

'What? That's bad news. If it's true.'

'You didn't know? Hadn't had a whisper?'

'Why should I?'

'Well, there was some talk . . . I mean, I thought maybe you were close enough to the family to . . . well . . .'

'The old Brigade grapevine seems to be rotting badly at the roots,' said Nick. 'You're way out of date.'

He was moving dismissively up towards his office when Compton added: 'Oh, and there was another message. Sounded like a young lady.' He fished a slip of paper from his pocket. 'Name of . . . er . . . Ariadne?'

Nick stopped dead. 'What did she say?'

'That you must call her urgently. Tonight at eight o'clock.' Compton handed over the note. 'It's a Cyprus number. She said you'd know the code.'

18

On the road above Limonia Bay Nick took out the map he had bought at the airport and tried to match it to the directions Ariadne had hurriedly dictated over the phone. A ruined temple above a huddled little village looked idyllic in the warm haze. Lots of places along the road had looked just as picturesque, locked in a time warp. The passer-by had no way of knowing what went on indoors.

The whole journey had been unreal. The abrupt contrast between Heathrow and the hot, dry landscape of Cyprus under its cloudless sky made Nick doubt whether he was still in a comprehensible world. Things were happening so fast, but against a background of timeless languor. It was all two-dimensional scenery from a travel brochure, in which it was impossible to visualize real people living out workaday lives.

The temple, when he found it, was a skeletal ruin of sand-coloured pillars above the dusty green of a vineyard. Ariadne came from behind an ancient column, her light grey dress clinging to her in the heat, her arms and shoulders bare. As he drew closer, she stared longingly at him, then skipped away around another column like some classical nymph who might briefly taunt a human before disappearing into the harsh blue sky.

He caught up with her and put his arms round her. It was a long time before either of them spoke. At last he said: 'We'd better get going.'

Still clinging to him, there was nothing ethereal about her now. Then she loosened her grip and again looked him searchingly in the face. 'Why did you come here?'

He was taken aback. 'Because you asked me. You begged me to come.'

She tossed her head. 'I do not beg. And anyway, in the circumstances . . .'

'What circumstances?' When she pulled herself away from him and leaned over the wall to stare into the distance, he said: 'I don't know why I had to come here at all. If you wanted to leave Petros, why didn't you just jump on a plane?'

'I had to talk to you first.'

'About what?'

'Oh, nothing. If you don't understand . . .'

'No, I don't.'

She was beginning to weep, her shoulders

hunching into a graceful curve. Nick strode towards her and seized her arm. She let out a cry of pain. When he turned her arm, he could see where its creamy golden smoothness was marred by an ugly purple weal.

'Where did you get that? Petros?' Mutely she nodded. 'He suspects something?'

'Suspicion – he is nothing but suspicion and arrogance. But he isn't sharp enough to know you're here. Not yet. I waited until I was sure which day he would be over to his precious mother's farm again. What about in London?'

Nick shrugged. Who would he have told? Certainly not the family, who in any case were not on speaking terms with him.

He wondered how the family would cope when he and Ariadne got back. If they did both get back.

'Look, we can't hang around. You're all set to leave with me right now?'

'No, there's a problem. Petros has taken my passport from me. He must have thought I might try to leave him.'

'That's useful. Any idea where it is?'

'In a safe deposit box in the bank.'

'Oh, no.'

'It's not too awful. I've been watching him to see where he keeps the key. If I can get it, they know me in the bank, they'll give me access.'

'Unless he's told them not to.'

'No, I don't think so. It would hurt that pride of his to let bank clerks get even a hint of a problem with his wife.'

'His pride doesn't stop him hurting that wife.'

She laughed ruefully; but then she was caught up in more of her eager plans. 'Tomorrow morning he will be working on the vines, so he won't need his keys. As soon as he goes out I'll get the deposit box key and meet you outside the bank with my things. I'll bring very little – only what I can carry. You have the car at the bank, and then we get to the airport. Tomorrow!' she breathed.

That was not quite the way Nick had wanted it to turn out. He had hoped she would be here ready and waiting to fly off without delay. He had booked the flight, and was due back on duty tomorrow. But Ariadne was in no mood to listen to anything about the Brigade or his responsibilities. He would have to change the flight, and make a call to London to plead sick, or something.

'Hanging about another day,' he ventured, 'we're taking a big risk.'

'I'll see you outside the bank tomorrow.' There was no dismaying her now. 'You can see the town from here. Be in the square by ten, and I'll be out as soon as I can.'

'I'll stay at the Limonia Bay Hotel. If you can manage it, ring me when you're on your way to the bank.'

She clung to him, kissed him again and again,

and then slid away between the ancient pillars.

Her fragrance and the sheer throbbing life of her clung exquisitely to him after she had gone; but he found himself dazed, wondering exactly what he was doing.

That night was hot and airless. The slowly revolving fan did little to help. He was dripping with sweat as he lifted the phone and got through to Blackwall and Station Officer Suffolk. 'Harry, book me out on an emergency P.H. tomorrow, will you? And tell John Hallam the moment he gets in.'

'All right, mate. Nothing seriously wrong, is there?'

'Just a bit of family business. Caught me by surprise. I'll be back the day after.'

'Here, where are you? This is a dreadful line.'

'I'm in a call-box. Must go, there's somebody waiting. Just book that P.H., right?'

He didn't know what Harry Suffolk would make of it. And right now he didn't much care.

George Green was heading for the locker room as Station Officer Suffolk closed the office door and came down the stairs. George tried to step aside, but Suffolk said: 'Look, George, it's time one of our lot made it clear to you. We all know how you must be feeling about Jaffa. But as far as I'm concerned, if you take over someone's duty you take whatever comes with it, including the risks. I know Jaffa will say the same when we get him out of there.'

George nodded glumly, and tried to go on his way, but Suffolk blocked him.

'George. I don't know if you've heard, but the Brigade's organizing this fund-raising event for a charity, R.A.F.T. They help victims of burns like Jaffa's. And do research into plastic surgery, that sort of thing.'

'The hospital's hoping he won't need anything like that.'

'No, I know. But it's just that part of this event is a raft race.'

'We've had Wendy-house charities for kids, trips to Euro-Disney. Raft races now?'

Suffolk pressed home the possible interest. 'White Watch are putting up a team. Just thought your mob might be interested as well. I've put the details on the board in the mess.' He slapped George on the back. 'Start asking around, eh?'

George went on into the mess, read the notice on the board, and drew attention to it as the others filtered in. It was the least he could do. Still it wasn't enough, and he would still have preferred to turn back the clock and cancel the whole horror story out altogether. But maybe there were things that could be patched up, things that could contribute.

Sally Reid was the immediately practical one. 'Where do we get a raft from?'

'We make one.'

'Just out of things we find?' said Recall. 'Like an old bathtub?'

'We could use Kevin's houseboat,' suggested Billy. 'That's an old tub.'

'Watch it.'

Out of all the insults and throwaway remarks, a pattern began to emerge.

By the end of the watch, George was becoming infected by the mere idea of it. Jokes apart, he began to build a raft in his head, knowing where he could scrounge materials and where he could lean on people until they put their hands in their pockets. He had to believe in it: simply had to be Blue Watch's prime mover.

He took a roundabout route home, calling on all the old acquaintances he could locate to drum up support for the charity. When he got in, he called 'Sorry I'm late, love,' but got no reply. Kelly had the radio turned up so loud that she could probably not hear him. He went on into the sitting-room and said it again: 'Sorry I'm late.'

Kelly was looking even more heavily pregnant than when he went out this morning, spearing a pickled onion from an almost empty jar. She was not even aware of his arrival until he leaned over to kiss her.

'I've been out getting sponsorship for a new charity idea the lads have dreamed up for Jaffa.'

'Oh, yes? Where was that, then – up West?'

'No, local. What'd be the point of wandering round the West End?'

'You weren't at your theatre again, then? Seeing Larissa?' Kelly ground the name out as if it were some kind of insult she had only just acquired.

George flinched, then said as smoothly as he could manage: 'I told you, that job's over. The company's gone home. What's this Larissa stuff?'

Kelly heaved herself upright in an ungainly wriggle. 'Oh, don't tell me you've forgotten her already?'

'What are you on about?'

'This.'

She dug down into the couch behind her, and hurled the ballet souvenir programme across the room at him. He must have thrown it down casually when he got home that last night. It didn't seem as if there ought to be much to explain about it. 'It's a programme signed by the cast. Nice crowd. So what?'

'So what?' she echoed furiously. 'So what about page seven?'

George had not even gone through the programme in any detail. Now he flipped over the pages, past the signatures of all the others, and arrived at the half-page photograph of Larissa at her most aloof and pensive. Beside it there was a scrawled note. Under Kelly's venomous gaze he read it with a sinking heart. *My dear, brave George, you were my first and only friend in London. I will miss you and look forward to when we can meet again. Please do not forget me. I send you my love. Larissa.*

'Well?' demanded Kelly.

'Well, so what? You know what these people are like. She's a stranger. A foreigner. They get all soppy, don't they?' He felt himself a traitor even as he spoke, cheating on an ideal even though Larissa was far away and he would never see her again and it couldn't matter now. 'What d'you think I'm going to do? Move to Russia and become a ballet dancer?'

If he had been hoping to provoke a smile, he was disappointed. Kelly said: 'Why not? I don't care if you do.' She stumbled to her feet and blundered towards the bedroom.

'Look, this is crazy. I put out a fire in her dressing-room, that was all. So I'm a hero. But after that, nothing happened. And what's the point in you getting worked up over nothing?'

'George, you're a fireman. You should know that there's no smoke without fire.'

She thudded the bedroom door shut behind her.

The sun beat down on the roof of the hire car. Nick leaned his elbow on the edge of the open window, trying to play the jaded tourist under the gaze of a number of elderly men blinking drowsily outside the tavern.

Just when he thought he could bear it no longer,

Ariadne came stepping gracefully out of the bank on the far side of the square. She held a passport high and waved it triumphantly at Nick. As she moved towards the car, an elderly lady came along the pavement, calling 'Ariadne!' and beginning to talk animatedly in local Cypriot dialect. Nick caught only a few phrases, but his heart sank. Somehow this threatened trouble. He sounded his horn impatiently and leaned over to open the passenger door. Ariadne flung herself in. Even as she slammed the door he was accelerating away in a cloud of dust.

'Who was that?'

'Petros's aunt.'

'Oh, great. That's all we need.'

Along the unfamiliar twisting roads he kept his foot clamped down all the way between lemon groves and scatterings of sun-baked houses, sharing his attention between the route ahead and his rear-view mirror.

They reached the airport. He did not wait to sign off the car, but left it outside the hire office with the keys still in the ignition as he and Ariadne dashed through check-in with minutes to spare. Not until they were airborne did they both lean back in their seats, gasping and laughing nonsensically. As the plane tilted in a wide arc, they could see cars below them racing along the approach roads to the airport. Ariadne strained to see if one was Petros's; but in a matter of seconds they had all become too diminutive to identify.

Nick closed his eyes and tried to predict in his head what would be waiting for them in London.

He half expected to find a squad of thugs in the alley beside his block of flats. Or maybe outside the flat itself, ready and waiting. But there was nobody about as he opened the door and went in, reaching for the light switch.

Well, they had made it.

Ariadne went past him into the living-room, tossing her coat across the sofa and kicking off her shoes. Nick put their cases down in the hallway and slowly followed her in.

'Well,' she exulted, 'here we are, then.'

When he stopped in the middle of the floor, not used to the idea of her presence here from now on – permanently here, part of his life because he had travelled hundreds of miles to bring her into it – she threw her arms wide and hurried towards him.

Yes, they had made it. Here they were.

19

The weather made quite a change from Cyprus. In the grey morning light Ariadne stood by the window, staring pensively out through the drizzle. Nick finished packing his kit and came to stand beside her. He knew she wanted him to stay. The excitement and tension of the escape and return, and the ecstatic frenzy of the night hours, were giving way to cool, everyday reality. On her first day back she needed the reassurance of having him beside her every minute, until they were quite sure what was going to happen.

But there was one sure thing that had to happen. He had to be on duty at Blackwall. He had booked that one emergency P.H. through Station Officer Suffolk; but one more day, and he would be absent without leave. There would be no way of covering for that.

'Don't answer the phone.' He put his arm round

her. She had been so strong so far. Last night she had been wild and supple and joyful. Now she sensed how vulnerable she felt. 'Don't answer the door. But there are spare keys on the hook there, if you do want to go out.'

'I'll be all right, Nick.' It was cool and steady, but little more than a whisper. 'I know where everything is.'

'Right, then.'

He kissed her as though they had been married for years and this was the thousandth time he had done it before setting out on another routine day at the office.

Blackwall Fire Station was a welcome sight. Whatever problems might arise today, they would be far less tricky than the ones he had saddled himself with at home. It had all seemed so imperative at the time, with the adrenalin surging and lifting him to an exhilarating, drunken high. Now he was sober again.

'Morning, guv.' Billy Ray's inquisitive eyes followed him eagerly across the yard to the rear doors.

'Morning, Billy.' He was halfway up the stairs as Station Officer Suffolk came down, ready to knock off. 'Thanks for your help, Harry.'

'Think nothing of it. You can do the same for me one day. A pity you can't swap me a touch of that suntan right now.'

John Hallam was waiting at the top of the stairs.

'Morning, guv. Everything all right?' He wasn't so obviously nosey as young Billy, but there was more than a hint of curiosity behind the question.

'Fine, thanks,' said Nick flatly. 'Good. You had a call from Bulstrode's P.A. yesterday. Didn't say what it was. Wants you to call him back.'

'Right.' There might be something helpful in this. If his promotion was going through, he might be able to take Ariadne away from this region, shake all the dust of rumour and personal involvements off their shoulders, and start afresh.

'Oh, and one thing, guv. You haven't seen Sicknote yet, have you?'

'No. Why?'

'Don't laugh when you do. He's wearing a wig.' Before Nick could think of any possible answer to this improbable idea, Hallam went on: 'Not a full rug, just a bit on top. I've had a look at regs, and apparently it's all right, as long as it's fireproof.'

'Are you pulling my leg?'

'No, guv. He came in with it yesterday. Thinks we haven't noticed. Nobody wants to spoil the joke yet.'

Nick would have bet on that. The gang would keep it going for as long as they could, and then heaven only knew how they would finish it off.

The bells sounded for roll-call.

Each familiar sound was a steadying influence. John Hallam's voice droned out as measured and predictable as ever: ' . . . and Firefighter Green.

Riders on the pump ladder are myself, Firefighter Wilson driving, Firefighter Quigley, Firefighter Medhurst, Firefighter Mackenzie, and Firefighter Ray. Watch detailed, sir.'

'Carry on, sub.'

'Blue Watch' – the timing never varied – 'Blue Watch, 'shun. For your duties, fall out.'

Nick had difficulty in keeping his eyes off Bert Quigley's helmet and wondering what would be revealed when he took it off.

Around ten o'clock Nick sauntered down to the mess. He usually waited for Bayleaf or Billy to bring him a coffee in his office, but today he was restless. He needed the continued reassurance of the familiar pattern, the repeated jokes and snide squabbles. Today he walked into a discussion which baffled him. Something had obviously started up in his absence.

'Quite sure we're all organized for Friday?' Bayleaf was asking.

'There's a full set of rules in the office.' George was sitting glumly with his head down, for once not rustling his way through the sports pages.

'Who's paddling this thing anyway?' demanded Sally. 'Be like moving an oil rig if we all get on it.'

'Has to be six. Four to row, two to launch.'

Nick made his way to the hatch and took the opportunity of edging past Sicknote and glancing down at the strange fuzz on his pate. Even through this covering Sicknote seemed to sense he was being inspected, and glanced sharply up. Nick looked away and said: 'George, how're things with your wife? Any minute now, isn't it?'

'They'll take her in next week, if it hasn't happened by then.'

'What's she want this time, boy or a girl?'

'Hard to tell,' said George dourly. 'Different husband, probably.'

The argument surged up again.

'Four, then, with you,' said Bayleaf. 'Who else?' He glanced at Recall. 'You're game for a good cause, right?'

Recall sighed. 'Can't swim. But I'll be a launcher.'

'Right.' Bayleaf turned his attention to Billy. 'And just right for you, your size. Not too much ballast.'

'No, I've forgotten how to swim.'

'That's all right, you can drown.'

'Anyway, we know Sally can swim.' Kevin moved warily close to her. 'And *I'm* getting my master's ticket soon.'

Nick could stand it no longer. 'Will someone kindly fill me in on what this is all about?'

Hallam came to the rescue. 'Sorry, guv. A charity raft race, next Friday. In aid of the R.A.F.T. burns charity. Felt it was the least we could do.' He was carefully not looking at George. Nick got the message. The Watch were making a sort of ritual offering in honour of Jaffa. And George was still feeling guilty.

'Right.'

'I gather, guv, that there'll be a senior officers' team competing.'

'Will there, now?' In reply to Sicknote's challenging stare he said: 'I'm not a senior officer.' And added silently: *Not yet*.

As he headed for the door, Sally had turned on Sicknote. 'What's holding *you* back? Don't want to get your hair wet?'

'I wouldn't mind. Just don't want to stand in anybody else's way, that's all.'

Hallam said: 'Ought to give Geoff a chance: keep it fair.'

'Who wants Geoffrey on board?' asked Sally. 'Anyone?'

Nick made himself scarce, but before he could reach his office, the bells went down.

Kevin was dashing out with the message. 'Fire and explosion, Crotlet Road. Both.'

Teams for the two appliances dashed into positions established by the sub at roll-call. The pump, with Sally at the wheel, was first away with its blues and two-tones flashing and blaring. The pump ladder swung out a couple of hundred yards behind. Nick settled himself into the seat beside Sally and watched the streets flashing past, the heads turning. Way back in this job he had found himself sitting tensed up, driving, as it were, for the driver. Now, at ease with the skills of Bayleaf, George Green or Sally, he was content to conserve his energies for what lay ahead.

Smoke was rising above a street of small terraced houses. A young woman was struggling with two others on the corner of an alley leading to the back of the row, as if determined to dash back into the flames of her kitchen. Nick sprang down from the pump, waving Recall and Geoff Pearce to ready the hose equipment. He took one look at the young woman's scorched forehead and some deep, bleeding gashes down her cheeks, and snapped: 'Sally, first-aid. And call an ambulance.' As the pump ladder came hot in pursuit down the street, he yelled and waved at the scattering of gaping onlookers to get well clear to the other side of the street, and then headed for the woman still threshing hysterically between her two neighbours.

'Tell me who's in the house, madam. How many?'

'Keith, my husband.' She was letting out a high, screaming breath between each syllable. 'In the kitchen.'

'What are we dealing with? Gas cooker, or – '

'He'd been working on a formica tabletop. Must have been the fumes.'

'Molly was just coming back from shopping,' said one of her friends. 'And she must have – '

'Keith was lighting the gas to make some tea when he saw me,' squealed Molly, 'and there was this bang – and everything . . . God, he's in there, you've got to – '

'What was he working with?'

'You've got to get him out. He was on fire, he – '

'My men are round there already,' said Nick in the calmest tone he could muster. 'It's important to let them know what they're facing. You said something about fumes. What was your husband working with?'

'There was some sort of glue he got from the D.I.Y. store, I know that, but I don't know . . .' She was sobbing uncontrollably again as the notes of an approaching ambulance came round the corner.

Some sort of glue, thought Nick: and ten to one he hadn't read the instructions about not leaving tins of adhesive open in an unventilated room.

He hurried towards the alley, calling up to Bayleaf in the pump ladder cab. 'Bayleaf, make it "Persons Reported".'

'Guv.'

Kevin and Recall were getting rigged up in their B.A.'s. Nick followed George Green, crouching to hurry through the clouds of smoke in the back yard. George reached what was left of the shattered kitchen window, shards of which must have been responsible for the wife's lacerated face, and peered in. 'I can see him. He's on the floor in there.'

'Hold it. Don't do any . . . *George!*'

George squared up to the kitchen door, poised

himself, and gave one mighty kick which thrust it inwards. A fresh gush of smoke enveloped him. Nick bellowed another order, but George had disappeared. When he came backing out he was easing a blackened, inert figure into the open. Nick stooped to help, and together they lifted the man as gently as possible towards the alley. Recall and Billy swung a hose round behind them and set to work on the blazing interior.

Molly howled again as she saw her husband being laid carefully on the ground. 'Keith! Please . . .' Heedless of her own injuries, she was staring in horror at the singed hair, scorched clothing, and blistered face, wanting to touch him but terrified of doing so in case he crumbled to powder under her hand. John Hallam held her arm firmly until her friends could regain control, and looked past her at the station officer. 'Any more in there, guv?'

'No, that's it. Two in for a search, though. And hang about for any bull's-eyes that might flare up again.'

'He's in shock,' panted George. 'He's stopped breathing.'

He was down on his knees as the ambulance edged carefully into the alley entrance. His mouth-to-mouth technique had been practised often enough, not just in training but in reality, and he went at it methodically; but this time Nick could sense there was something personal at stake. It might have been Jaffa lying there at death's door. He had to be brought back: *had* to be.

Suddenly Keith's body shook as if jolted by an electric shock, and he began to mumble back against George's mouth.

'Nice work, George,' said Nick quietly. 'You got him.'

Two paramedics took over, and Keith was moved gently into the ambulance. When they were well out of earshot, Nick said: 'Warm in there, was it? You didn't hear me?'

'Hear what, guv?' said George innocently.

There was a cheer from a window above, as Kevin and Sally leaned out. Nick and George exchanged a narrow grin of mutual understanding.

'I'll put it down to the heat of the moment, shall I?' said Nick. 'But don't go quite that deaf again. You might fail your next medical.'

It was two days since they had driven off in search of Trevor, but the memory of it still rankled. Bayleaf went through the day's duties automatically, getting everything right from instinct rather than by concentration. He was stuck here; still trapped in familiar routines. His mind still wandered back, bruised, to the end of their high hopes.

It had taken only a few hours to confirm the worst. Driving grimly down towards the Sussex coast without turning his head to look at Clare's set features, or at the features of the countryside which had once seemed so attractive, Bayleaf said: 'So we're listening to no more arguments, right? We make it clear to him that we're dissolving the partnership.'

'And this time,' said Clare frigidly, 'don't let him talk you round.'

They were both tense as they drove into the caravan park and walked across to hammer on the door of Trevor's caravan, nerving themselves for a stand-up row. There was no answer. Clare dragged the step-up from the door to one of the windows, and peered inside. There was nobody there.

'Nothing at all,' she reported. 'It's been completely emptied.'

'The bastard.'

They drove to the restaurant itself. It was as gutted and deserted as the caravan. The power was off. In the gloom of the interior Bayleaf picked up yet another envelope he was afraid to open. When he did summon up the courage, it turned out to be a contractor's bill which meant nothing to him.

Clare had to go out to phone: the connection here must have been cut off ages ago. In her absence, Bayleaf found another bill and a threatening letter. He paced about despondently until she got back.

'Kids all right?'

'Yes, Melanie's getting their tea.' She looked at the crumpled scraps of paper he was still clutching between his fingers. As he sank on to a packing case, she pulled another box over and sat facing him. 'We're not going to see Trevor again, you know.'

'Just as well. I'd be done for murder.'

This was the end of the line. Trevor had done a runner. The office was closed, his caravan was deserted, the builders had not heard a word from him, and everywhere there seemed to be unpaid bills. They were just going to have to sit down with Mr Philby, present him with all the documents and invoices and tax demands and let him sort out what they ought to do next: how much they were liable for, and how much they might salvage.

Clare said it out loud: 'We're not going to get a penny back, you do realize that? It's more a question of how much more we're going to be clobbered for.'

'Well, I think we'll wait for an expert opinion on that.'

'Shame you didn't say that when we first got into this.'

'What d'you mean? It was all drawn up by a solicitor.'

'Not quite,' said Clare angrily. 'If you remember, Trevor claimed it was drawn up by his solicitor. Did we ever meet him?'

'Well, no, but it must be kosher, the agreement. Old Philby said it was legal. What else could we have done?'

'We could've done what I said in the first place, which was not to go into business with Trevor.'

'So now it's all my fault.'

'No, it's mine as well, for ever letting you talk me into putting my money – the *boys'* money – into this poxy dump.' She got up. 'Mike, you've got to face up to it. We have been well and truly ripped off, and now we're in it up to our necks.'

He hardly had the willpower to get up on his feet. When he reached out for her, speechless but wanting to hold her and somehow set things right between them, she angrily shrugged him off.

It looked as if it would have to be Blackwall for a few more years yet.

Unlike the taciturn Bayleaf, the rest of the crews of the two appliances were in tolerably good spirits when they got back to Blackwall. A few quips about Geronimo and some flash behaviour were tossed amiably at George's head; and at last he summoned a smile. After Geoff Pearce had booked them back in, Nick was about to go and phone A.C.O. Bulstrode when Pearce said: 'Looks like we've got company, sir.'

A large blue Mercedes had swung on to the station forecourt. It was certainly no Brigade vehicle. Several pairs of eyes studied it with growing interest as Nick, a sudden chill gripping his stomach, went out of doors again. He heard Recall mutter: 'Friends of his?'

'Don't look exactly friendly, do they?'

Yanni was looking far from friendly. His dark

face had gone several thunderous shades darker as he got out, with a brawny shape shadowing him. Nick recognized Spiros, never acknowledged as a bodyguard – why should an honest businessman like his Uncle Yanni need a bodyguard? – but never made light of or joked with even by close friends of the family. The driver, not many sizes smaller, also got out of his seat.

Nick was relieved that he could keep his voice so cool and authoritative. 'You'll have to move that, sir. You're on Brigade property.' When Yanni made no move, he added: 'Right now, if you would.'

Yanni's voice was by no means as steady. 'You steal a man's wife, and she hides now from her family. You're a big man, eh?'

From the corner of his eye Nick was aware of George Green moving casually forward, like a footballer marking Spiros. To all appearances he ignored him; but was sneakingly glad of George's presence.

'You're also obstructing the appliances,' he said. 'Move the car, sir, will you?'

'You know what you are, both of you. And so do we.'

'Fine. Now if you'll – '

'No use to anybody.' There was a contempt in Yanni's tone which bit more hurtfully than any threat would have done. 'So her husband gives her to you. And I come to tell you that I give her to you. She is yours.'

'That's right,' said Nick evenly. 'Now will you remove the vehicle, sir, or do we have to do it?'

There was a moment of silent stand-off. Nick was conscious of the Watch assembling behind him. Spiros and Yanni's driver sized them up. Then the three men got back into the car. As it drove away, Nick turned back towards the station to find that the Watch were swiftly dispersing as if anxious to catch up with their duties.

In his office he phoned Lewisham, and then called Hallam in. 'John, take charge for an hour, will you? Get Kevin to do the nominal boards. Apparently A.C.O. Bulstrode's getting impatient to see me.'

On the way there he tried to rid his mind of all the sour upsets and uncertainties, and prepare himself for some bright certainties. Promotion . . . change of scenery . . . there had to be *something* in the wind. Bulstrode's repeated calls must mean that he wanted to break the good news to him personally, and soon.

He had not been prepared to find the A.C.O. in a civilian suit and tie. It was more formal than the clothes Bulstrode had worn that unforgettable evening when Nick had been faced with him in Diana's home; but still it seemed unnatural to find the man's bulky frame out of the imposing uniform.

'Come in, Georgiadis. Do sit down.' His gaze

was still on a framed group photograph on the wall behind his desk. 'Thirty years ago. Hmph. Where did it all go, eh?'

Nick knew this was a moment for diplomacy. 'It's a good record, sir.'

'Your predecessor there, in front of me. Good man, Sidney Tate – good officer.'

'Yes, sir, so I understand.'

'Keeps bees now. Can't see me getting on with bees, somehow.' He tore himself away from the photograph and stooped to open a desk drawer. 'Like a drink, Georgiadis? Little retirement libation with me?'

'I'm on duty, sir.'

'So am I. Not for much longer, though. Come on, it's an order. Show some respect.'

Nick waited until the whisky had been poured and the glass was in his hand before saying: 'You were talking of possible retirement last time we met, sir, but I didn't know it was definite.'

'It is now. And I sent for you because I thought I'd enlighten you on a Brigade decision. Call me old-fashioned, but since it concerns you I think you ought to know about it. The truth, I mean, not the handouts. No skin off my nose, anyway. I'm off. After thirty years I'd rather jump than be pushed. I might be a dinosaur, but I do have my dignity.' He must already have had a few glasses to be teetering on such an unsteady, maudlin edge. 'I do have my dignity.'

'Yes, sir.' Nick waited a few moments and then probed: 'This decision, sir. What exactly is it?'

'Reconstruction.' It came out as a sudden snarl. 'That's what it's all about. Reconstruction. The buzz-word these days. Don't hear much plain English any more, do we?'

'No, sir. But I'm afraid I don't follow, sir. How does it concern me?'

Bulstrode took another massive gulp of whisky as if to summon up courage to go on, which was so unlike him as to be distressing. 'Because in plain English, Georgiadis, you're stuck where you are. At least for now. You applied for promotion, and there was no damn reason why you shouldn't have got it. No reason at all. Then, lo and behold, it's reconstruction. Reconstruction!' This time it had become a resounding curse. 'Current promotion round cancelled, ask me not why. They don't tell me – I'm retiring, so I don't need to know. Retiring. While you, Georgiadis, are stuck, I'm afraid. Plain enough?'

'Yes, sir.' It took such a short few seconds to destroy hope and cast a cloud over what had seemed a sunny future. He forced himself to say: 'Thank you for letting me know.'

'Nothing much to thank me for. I know that, Georgiadis. I also know what it's like waiting to hear. I thought I'd spare you any more of it, that's all.'

'I appreciate that, sir.'

He did appreciate it; but the cloud did not lift.

There was a tap at the door, and a familiar figure came in. District Officer Scase, importantly carrying a folder, cast a disapproving glance at Nick and at the two whisky glasses.

'Yes?' barked Bulstrode.

'The itinerary for the Home Office Inspectorate that you requested, sir.' Scase laid the folder reverently on the desk. 'I've detailed it myself, sir. I think you'll find it's all in order. Visits, times, transport, refreshments. I've added a note of my own, about the – '

'All right, man, all right. I can read. No doubt it's a model of its kind.' Bulstrode rooted in his drawer and produced another glass. 'Come on, have a farewell toast with me while you're here.'

'I don't touch alcohol, thank you, sir. On duty or off it.'

Scase shot another critical glance at Nick, who pretended not to notice. Bulstrode, though, was in no mood to feign indifference. 'Of course. I should have known, shouldn't I? I don't suppose you even fart in the bath, D.O. Scase, do you?'

'I beg your pardon, sir?'

'If you're a vision of the future, Scase, I'm glad I won't be here to see it. Reconstruction! You'd make a beehive look like a bunch of wandering hippies, with this managerial mania of yours. This service has always been about fighting fires, not filling up another form.' He gestured towards the photograph. 'Ask Sidney Tate. Ask any of those men in that picture there. They were firefighters, Scase. I don't know what the hell you are.'

Tight-lipped, Scase said: 'I think it's best I say nothing just now, sir. Will that be all?'

'Yes, that'll be all. I don't want to say anything I might regret. I might not sleep at night, hmph? Go on, off you go, D.O. Scase.' When the door had closed behind the hapless D.O., Bulstrode heaved a happy sigh and patted his stomach like a man who had just slackened off a couple of notches in his belt. 'Shouldn't have done that. But I rather enjoyed it. How was it for you, Georgiadis?'

Nick raised his glass. Its contents weren't the only spirits which had lifted. 'Have a good retirement, sir. You've earned it.' He finished his drink, and at the door looked back to say: 'I liked the bit about the bees!'

When the door had closed behind him he seemed still to hear Bulstrode chuckling with delight. But once again his own euphoria was short-lived. Bulstrode, as the A.C.O. himself had said, was the past. Scase was the future.

He must shake off this mood before he returned home to Ariadne.

It was an idea that would take some getting used to: home, with Ariadne.

20

It had begun in the office, and then slyly continued in the coffee bar across the way. At first Sandra had not been too perturbed by Mr Robinson leaning over her while ostensibly studying her computer screen; and had thought his remarks in the coffee bar no more than flippant. It was the way people put on an act to relieve the tedium of office life.

'Hello, Sandra, don't mind if I join you? I think I can squeeze in.'

He had proceeded to do just that, pressing himself against Sandra's right hip. When he had settled on the neighbouring stool, his leg edged towards hers.

'I didn't realize you came here, Mr Robinson. I only found it myself yesterday.'

'Oh, I come here now and again. It's not bad. Call me Steven, anyway. We're not in the office now, are we?'

He ate half a sandwich before speaking again. Then he said casually: 'You're married, aren't you? Chap's something in the Fire Brigade, isn't he?'

'That's right. He's sub officer at Blackwall.'

'Takes some guts, that. I expect you're very proud of him. And happy?'

She wasn't sure what to make of this, but said: 'Yes. Of course.'

'I'm the same. Married, quite content to be. Don't want any upheavals, don't want to upset anyone. But . . .' He made a move to edge closer to her, but he was already as close as he could get. 'I like a change now and then, if you know what I mean. With someone who feels the same way. Just a bit of fun – don't want to rock any boats. I get the impression you're that sort of person, too.'

His hand wandered under the counter to her knee.

'Here, what are you doing?' She glanced around to see if anyone had noticed what was going on.

Robinson's hand slid away, but he was grinning as if they were accomplices now, misinterpreting her protest as being nothing more than a worry about the public. He glanced at his watch and eased himself off his stool.

'It can be anywhere you like, Sandra. Could do us both good, if you want it to. I mean' – there was a hint of an edge to his voice – 'me being your boss. Think about it, eh?'

He left her thinking about it.

'And the next thing I knew,' she told her audience around the Quigleys' coffee table, 'he was trying to lock us in.'

Jean Quigley, pushing a plate of her home-made biscuits along the table, was nodding as if this was just the sort of thing she would always expect of a man. Laura Mackenzie looked more and more the Scottish puritan by the minute. Clare Wilson seemed sunk in gloomy thought, abstractedly taking a biscuit but only half hearing what was going on around her. Sandra concentrated on Jean as the most receptive audience for her revelations.

She had not believed Robinson could have been so blatant. One lunchtime, when his secretary had already left to meet a boyfriend and Sandra was bent over her keyboard, intent on finishing a list of customers, he came and bent over her once more.

'In no hurry to satisfy your appetite, Sandra? Or maybe you're like me – different sort of appetite today, eh?'

'Just don't like to leave things in the air.' She completed the shut-down and headed for her coat and bag.

'No,' said Robinson. 'Nor do I. We were coming to an understanding in the coffee bar, weren't we? We could move on a bit, if you like.' He sauntered towards the door and turned the key in the lock. 'Won't be disturbed for a while.'

For a moment Sandra was robbed of breath. Then, as he came jauntily towards her, both breath and realization came back. She waited until Robinson was well within range, and then let fly. There was more strength in her right arm than she would have credited. She felt the gratifying shock up to her shoulder as her fist met Robinson's leering face. The sideways swipe sent him crashing over the end of her desk and on to the computer keyboard.

'And I told him,' she reported to the delighted Jean Quigley, 'that if he tried to put his paws on me again, he'd be talking in a very high voice when the police arrived.'

'How on earth did you get on with him afterwards?'

'I didn't. I quit right there and then. No way was I going to be regarded as a permanent fixture once he'd screwed me to the desk.'

Laura looked even more disapproving.

'Mind you,' Sandra admitted, 'it's not going to look too good on my C.V. when I go for another job – "Left because of refusal to sleep with the boss".'

'What are you going to do?'

'Spend more time with my family, as they say. But not too long. Think I'll try temping. It means I can quit any place any time I get suspicions about the boss or anybody else. And I can be more flexible in the hours. There's quite a good agency in the shopping precinct, and they're probably used to giving advice about male fantasists.'

'Speaking of fantasists' – Jean decided she had

had a non-speaking part for too long – 'my Bert has gone one stage further. It's not just hair restorer now – it's a wig.'

Laura brightened up. 'Oh, I'd heard about that.'

'Ah.' Jean was delighted. 'From Stuart? I *knew* it. Bert's been telling me that nobody's noticed, but I knew darn well that that lot wouldn't let it pass.'

'Oh, but that's not the game this time. Instead of taking the mickey with cracks about rugs and barnets and that sort of thing, they *are* letting it pass: deliberately not mentioning it. Stuart thinks that makes it even worse for Sicknote . . . er, Bert.'

'Pathetic lot, aren't they? Do you think we'll ever drag our husbands out of that establishment for half-baked delinquents?'

Laura said: 'I've been wondering about that. Since the kids had that holiday in Scotland with their grandmother, they look so well. I've got a hankering to go back up there myself – get away from London, lead a decent life in lovely surroundings.'

'What would Stuart do in Scotland?' asked Sandra.

'Wear a kilt?' suggested Jean.

Laura giggled. 'Have to be the Black Watch.'

'Honestly, you're getting as bad as them! Definitely time for a move.' Sandra glanced at Clare. 'You ought to be looking more cheerful, anyway. At least Mike's decided to take the plunge. Do we get invitations for cheap off-season breaks and free helpings of sea air as soon as you've headed down there?'

Clare nibbled at her last shred of biscuit. 'The way things are shaping up, we'll be lucky not to be heading for the bankruptcy court.'

They all turned towards her, not understanding. But before she could explain, Sandra waved at the clock and said: 'Time we were moving down to the lido to watch our gallant lads push the boat out. Time and tide wait for no man. Or words to that effect.'

The day had dawned bright, with hardly a cloud in the sky; but such clouds as there were moved swiftly, driven by a strong westerly wind which by afternoon was shaking the trees and ruffling the surface of the water. Two officials fussed between the marquees which had been set up, one at each end of the lido. The Blue Watch team joined in the general mêlée of lowering the tailgates of trucks and unloading rafts on to the grass. Competitors tried to look confident and relaxed, chatting offhandedly as if the result were already a foregone conclusion.

Sicknote, less relaxed than the others, patted his wig and started up a wandering conversation in the hope of distracting attention from this.

'Is it true you're leaving us, Sally?'

'Afraid so.'

'Couldn't stand the brash masculinity all around you?'

'It was the deodorants,' said Sally. 'They gave me sinus trouble.'

Kevin finished tightening one of the ropes lashing an oil drum to the planking, and glanced shyly at her.

George Green said: 'What's brought this on then, Sal?' He assumed it had something to do with Kevin: something that hadn't worked out. George was getting sensitive to that sort of thing: very sensitive indeed.

But she said: 'It's my dad. He's ill. Too many fags over too many years. Don't really know how long he's got, but I've got to move back to Wembley and look after him.'

'Fathers expect a lot of you, don't they?' muttered Kevin.

She smiled at him. It was Sally's usual spontaneous, uncomplicated smile. Whatever the problems had been, they were of no concern any longer. She was facing up to other things now.

Geoff Pearce, eager to be on gossiping level with the lads, said: 'From what I hear, it looks like the guv'nor's not getting his promotion after all.'

'So we're stuck with Zorba?' Billy pulled a face. 'I bet he's well choked, mister career man.'

'So would I be, if I were him,' said Pearce. 'First setback he's had. Doesn't do a lot for the chances of the rest of us – anybody thought of that?'

'Yes,' said Recall, '*you* have.'

John Hallam, who they knew had been through this sort of thing himself, shrugged. 'All part of life's rich tapestry, Geoff. Stay where you are, do not pass go. You get used to it after a while.'

Pearce had ceased to listen. His attention had been caught by a couple arriving among the spectators on the high bank beside the nearer marquee. It was the man they had just been talking about – and with a slim, elegant woman on his arm.

Billy whistled faintly. 'So that's what all this hush-hush disappearing act has been about.'

'Not bad,' said Bayleaf. 'Probably worth the air fare.'

'Good luck to him,' said Hallam loyally.

'Right, you lot.' Recall pointed to the stewards, who were waving commands to the competitors. 'Time to head for glory.'

The raft teams had lined up their various surrealist assemblies of wood, oil drums and rope along a start line at one end of the lido. The canoes, surfboards and inflatable dinghies which usually skimmed over the lake had been drawn up on the banks out of harm's way. There was a delay, as if at the last moment everybody had lost any idea of what this was all about. Then the starter stepped to the water's edge.

The crack of his pistol was the signal for a score of pigeons and rooks to spray up like party poppers into the air. It was also the signal for the teams to shove and heave their rafts into the water. Sally, George, Kevin and Billy made up the crew, with Sicknote and Recall keeping the raft stable while the four scrambled aboard with their paddles.

'Which way's forward, then?' asked Billy dubiously.

'Doesn't much matter,' said George, 'so long as we all face the same way.'

The screeching of indignant birds was accompanied by shouts from the direction of the marquee, where wives, John Hallam and Bayleaf set themselves to out-bellow the supporters of the White and Red Watch teams. There was a moment when the encouragement faltered, as the raft ceased going ahead and began to describe a leisurely circle.

'Swing her round to starboard,' panted Kevin. 'Luff up, luff up!'

'You luff up,' said Billy: 'I'll stay sitting down.'

When George had adjusted his muscular thrust to those of the others, the Blue Watch raft straightened its course and took a sudden energetic leap forward. By the halfway buoy they were a good length ahead, helped largely by one competitor lurching across another's stern. Firefighters and wives ashore redoubled their own vocal efforts. Nick Georgiadis and the woman with him attached themselves to the edge of the group; but then edged away again as Geoff and Patti Pearce began making what they thought was an unobtrusive way towards them.

With a superhuman effort one of the rival teams pulled level with Blue Watch, and two of its paddles made a quick stab at Kevin's and Sally's blades. The clash and screech of tangled woodwork mingled with shouts of abuse from both sides. Sally broke the snarl-up by thrusting her paddle deeper under her opponent's, twisting sharply, and heaving him overboard into the water. As he tried to scramble back aboard , his weight tilted the raft, and the other three of the crew slid ungracefully down to join him in the lake. There was an outburst of cheering from the bank.

At the far end Sicknote and Recall were wading into the water. Their arms were outstretched as if to draw the Blue Watch raft to them by an invisible line. Then it scraped the bottom, the crew scrambled off, and the six of them carried the raft triumphantly up the short slope to the finishing marker.

Station Officer Suffolk was running round the perimeter of the lake. He did not waste any time congratulating them, but panted at George: 'Enough of that, mate. Better get your skates on.'

'What's up?'

'Message for you from Kelly's brother. Sounds a bit dischuffed. He's taken her in to have her baby. You want to be there or not?'

Damp and dishevelled, George took off as swiftly as the birds at the sound of the starter's pistol.

'Which leaves us one short for the next leg,'

Recall pointed out. 'And don't look at me. I can't swim. It says in the rules that – '

'All right, all right.'

The eyes of Kevin and Billy turned upon Sicknote.

'Oh, no,' he protested. 'I've already told you – '

'You'll be better than Recall, anyway,' said Kevin. 'You're lighter than he is. Come on – the water's lovely.'

'Very poor timing on Kelly's part, if you ask me,' grunted Sicknote.

They moved off towards the rest and changing area in the marquee, followed by Hallam and Bayleaf, but had hardly reached it when Suffolk reappeared.

'Don't tell me the stork's dropped us a news bulletin on its way back from the hospital?' said Bayleaf.

'No, no word yet. But I thought you'd like to know I've seen the finals list. Senior Officers' crew just gone through, on a penalty. And,' Suffolk added suggestively, 'Scase is one of 'em.'

Nobody said a word; but they all smiled in a reflective way, and each one of them began weighing the possibilities of some unexpectedly dramatic developments in the final heat.

As Sicknote reluctantly scrambled aboard the raft, he found John Hallam beside him.

'Hey, this is too many. Against the rules.'

Hallam was tucking something away in the

interstices of the bow. 'Sod the rules.' It was an uncharacteristic pronouncement from the sub. 'Right, where's that officers' tub?'

His added weight, together with Sicknote's poor performance with his paddle after George's strenuous efforts, was slowing them down. Blue Watch was lagging behind the first two rafts; but Hallam seemed unperturbed – quite happy, in fact, to let the officers' raft overtake them a few yards to port.

Kevin took a great heave on his paddle to turn their own vessel at an angle towards their neighbour.

'Come on – ramming speed!'

Hallam started digging out a selection of missiles from his cache. Before he could judge the right distance and elevation, he became aware that Scase was watching with growing alarm. However slow Scase had been on the uptake, another of his crew had been wider awake. A plump white bag came in a low parabola from the officers' raft, exploding a few inches from Sicknote and showering him with flour.

'I knew it! This is going to be a fracas.'

'That's enemy action,' said Hallam. 'Keep rowing – get us alongside.'

Another flour bomb landed and puffed out a white cloud. Then Hallam steadied himself on his knees against the wild pitching of the raft, raised a small hand-held extinguisher, and accurately deluged Scase with foam. But one of Scase's colleagues was quicker off the mark. He sprang from one raft to the other as Kevin yelled: 'Repel boarders!' Sicknote tried to fend him off with a paddle; but the officer grabbed his shoulder and tipped him into the water. Desperately Sicknote spluttered his way round to the stern of the enemy raft, anxious to get out of the water at all costs. Crouched above him, the vengeful Scase grabbed him by the hair to give him a ducking . . . and was left staring with horror at the scalp that had come away in his hand.

It took a horrific few seconds to dawn on him. 'It's a wig. You're wearing a wig.'

Floundering, Sicknote groped to reclaim it. With as much dignity as he could muster through a mouthful of lido water, he announced: 'It's not a wig, actually, it's a hairpiece.'

And when at last they all found their way ashore, to a rapturous or derisive reception, with jibes about busy beavers and a deadpan 'Are you training it?' Sicknote summoned up an even more dignified manner as he turned towards a grinning steward. 'I was under the impression that I was supporting a charity, not being made a laughing-stock in front of a crowd.'

Billy said: 'It's all right, Sicknote. Don't get mad. Just keep your hair on.'

Music started up from speakers outside one of the marquees. 'A Life on the Ocean Wave' swelled out across the water.

'Should have been "The Flying Dutchman",' said Sicknote, intent on restoring some semblance of authority. 'Bags of operatic passion out there.'

'Yeah. And up there.' Recall nodded towards the figures of their station officer and his companion, her arm through his and her head on his shoulder.

'Thought she'd gone off and married some Cypriot or something,' said Kevin.

'She did. But somehow he's got her back.'

'Like we said, grand opera stuff.' Recall struck a dramatic pose. 'Hero rescues her from the villain at the last minute, and they sing their bloody heads off and live happily ever after.'

'Oh, no, that's not the form.' Sicknote wagged his head knowledgeably. 'Opera never works out like that. Always ends up with the hero and heroine sprawling dead all over the stage.'

'Not what I'd call much of an evening out,' said Sally. 'Give me the Rolling Stones any day.'

'Cor, that's a bit old-fashioned, isn't it?'

They drifted away in search of families and friends, and the watching crowd began dispersing. Nick Georgiadis and Ariadne were eventually left alone, two still figures blending into one on the water's edge. They seemed lost in a world of their own until the clatter of marquee equipment being dismantled shook them awake, and they went off towards Nick's car.

* * *

Ariadne was on her way out of the shower, towelling her sleek, glistening shoulders, when the phone rang. Nick glared at it. There was nobody he wanted to hear from right now: not with Ariadne looking the way she did. But it went on ringing, and at last he lifted the receiver.

Ariadne watched him fondly as he nodded and said: 'No, not at all, I'm glad you did. Great. Thanks, John. I'll call him in the morning.' When he turned back towards her, he explained: 'John Hallam. George just phoned him. Kelly's had a daughter. He's still dancing round the hospital.'

'You do like to keep an eye on all your family, don't you?'

'I suppose they *are* a sort of family.'

'This . . . George and his wife. You said they've already got a boy?'

'Sean, yes.'

'Nice.' Ariadne towelled her arms and stomach, wandering contentedly about the room. 'Maybe we should also have a boy first, too.'

'Mm. A boy'd be good.' It took another minute or so before her faraway smile rang bells – quieter, subtler bells than he was used to. 'Hey . . .'

'Yes.' Still damp, she let the towel fall and clung to him. 'I'm going to have your baby. I hope it's a boy, too.'